Glubbslyme

Jacqueline Wilson

Illustrated by
Jane Cope

Oxford University Press

Oxford Melbourne Toronto

Oxford University Press, Walton Street, Oxford OX2 6DP
Oxford   New York   Toronto
Delhi   Bombay   Calcutta   Madras   Karachi
Petaling Jaya   Singapore   Hong Kong   Tokyo
Nairobi   Dar es Salaam   Cape Town
Melbourne   Auckland

and associated companies in
Beirut   Berlin   Ibadan   Nicosia

Oxford is a trade mark of Oxford University Press

British Library Cataloguing in Publication Data

Wilson, Jacqueline
Glubbslyme. (Eagle books)
I. Title   II. Series
823'.914[J]   PZ7

ISBN 0 19 271563 1

Set by Best-set Typesetter Limited
Printed in Hong Kong

One

'My Dad says this is a witch's pond,' said Rebecca.

Sarah didn't say anything. Rebecca wasn't sure she was listening. She was too busy experimenting with Mandy's lipstick. She drew a shiny pink smile on her face. Mandy had a shiny pink smile too.

'Can I have a go with your lipstick, Mandy?' asked Rebecca.

'No, use your own,' said Mandy.

Rebecca didn't have any lipstick. She had only ever used red ice lollies or red Smarties, and the results weren't very successful. She longed to try Mandy's real lipstick.

'You let Sarah borrow it, so why won't you let me?' said Rebecca, although she knew why.

'Sarah's my best friend,' said Mandy, and her shiny pink smile stretched.

Rebecca had always thought *she* was Sarah's best friend. They went round together at playtimes and passed little notes in lessons and got the giggles and told each other secrets. But that was at school. Now it was the holidays and Sarah seemed to want to spend most of her time with Mandy, just because they lived next door to each other.

Rebecca couldn't stand Mandy. Mandy didn't seem to think much of her either.

'Sarah's my best friend too,' said Rebecca. 'Sarah, did you hear, my Dad says this is a witch's pond.'

'What are you on about?' said Mandy. 'What are you, some sort of baby? Do you believe in big bad naughty witches then, little diddums?'

'No, of course I don't,' said Rebecca, going as pink as the lipstick. 'But there did used to be witches and my Dad says they used to duck them in this pond.'

'My Dad says. My Dad says. You don't half go on about your Dad. Who cares what your Dad says?' said Mandy.

Rebecca cared. She loved her Dad more than anyone in the whole world. She didn't have a Mum any more so Dad was especially important. She loved him even when he was cross because the shopping and the washing and the cooking needed doing and she didn't always feel like helping. She loved him even more when he was cheerful and they played daft games of noughts and crosses and made up stories and sang silly songs. She loved him most of all when they had a special day out together. They had once had a lovely jam sandwich picnic in the park, by the pond. Dad had told her all about the witches and Rebecca had been very interested.

Sarah and Mandy didn't seem at all interested.

'They weren't daft story-book witches with pointed hats and broomsticks,' said Rebecca. 'They were often just lonely or a bit loopy.'

'Like you, you mean', said Mandy, and Sarah giggled.

'And people picked on them and accused them of witchcraft and tortured them,' said Rebecca.

'What did they do to them then?' asked Mandy, brushing Sarah's short hair into a very modern style.

Dad hadn't gone into the torture part, but Rebecca invented a great deal because they were listening properly at last. Rebecca was very good at making up disgusting tortures and even Mandy looked impressed. Sarah kept making sick noises and perhaps it was no wonder her hair was now standing on end.

'So what happened to them?' Sarah asked. 'Did they die after all that torture?'

'No, I *told* you. I knew you weren't listening,' said Rebecca. 'They took them to this pond and then they did the water test. They tied their left

5

thumb to their right big toe and their right thumb to their left big toe —' Rebecca tried to demonstrate. She overbalanced on the grass and Mandy cackled, but she still had Sarah's attention. 'They tied them up in this sort of knot thing and then they threw them in the pond — splosh!' said Rebecca. 'And if they sank they were innocent. If they bobbed up again then they were guilty and they were taken away and *burned*.'

Sarah and Mandy sat still, blinking.

'You've got that wrong,' said Mandy.

'No I haven't,' said Rebecca.

'But that wouldn't be fair,' said Sarah. 'If you were innocent you'd sink and so you'd drown anyway.'

'I know. That's the point,' said Rebecca. 'That's why it was so awful to be a witch.'

'I wonder how many witches drowned in this very pond then?' said Sarah, leaning forward and staring at the murky water. She scratched her head worriedly and destroyed her new hairstyle.

'Look what you've done, you've mucked it up,' said Mandy, sighing. 'Come here and I'll do it again for you.'

'No, it's all right, I didn't think much of it actually,' said Sarah. 'Here, Becky, do you think they're still down there? All those witch bodies?'

'You bet,' said Rebecca, peering too. 'Here, what's that long whitish thing out in the middle?

6

You don't think it's a *bone*, do you?'

Sarah shrieked and clutched Rebecca. Mandy sighed. She gave herself another lipstick smile but it looked strained.

'I'm getting fed up with this park and its silly old pond,' she said. 'Let's go home, Sarah. Come over to my place and we can try out all my make up. My Mum's given me heaps of eye stuff and I've got my own Pretty Peach perfume.'

'I quite like it here,' said Sarah. 'You know, it *could* be a bone, and those little bits at the end — they're the fingers.'

'Yes! She probably died reaching out desperately, screaming for help.' Rebecca screamed too, waving her arms around violently.

'Watch out, you clumsy twit. And how could she wave her arms around? You said they were all tied up to her toes,' Mandy pointed out. 'You're just making it up, Rebecca. It's all fibs and lies.'

'No, it's not! Look, my Dad says —' ·

'My Dad says, my Dad says. She's starting to sound like a parrot. Can't you play another record, Parrot Face?'

'Don't call Becky silly names, Mandy, it gets on my nerves,' said Sarah.

Rebecca smiled. Sarah smiled back at her. Mandy stood up. She wasn't smiling. She glared at the pond. She went on glaring at it. And then she smiled after all.

7

'They couldn't have ever drowned witches in this pond,' she said triumphantly. 'It's not deep enough.'

'Yes it is,' said Rebecca.

'Yes it is,' said Sarah, but she sounded uncertain.

'It *isn't*. You look.' Mandy picked up a long stick, walked to the pond's edge, leaned right out and stuck the stick in the water. She banged it up and down on the bottom of the pond. A great deal of the twig stayed above water.

'There! It would barely come up to your knees. Are you sure it was witches? Sure it wasn't fairies? Fairy *stories*, more like.'

'My Dad says you can drown in only a few inches of water,' said Rebecca.

'My Dad says! Parrot face.'

Sarah didn't object this time.

'You can maybe drown someone, but you can't duck them,' she said. 'And it isn't deep enough, Becky.' She took the stick from Mandy and prodded vigorously all round the pond to prove it.

'It's deep enough in the middle,' said Rebecca. 'I know it is. They threw them into the *middle* of the pond.'

Sarah threw several stones into the middle.

'I don't think it's any deeper in the middle,' she said.

One of the stones hit the bony arm and it

8

waved. Sarah gasped but then she saw it was only an old branch of a tree with a twiggy bit at the end.

'I don't think this was ever a witch's pond,' she said.

'Of course it isn't. It's just an ordinary muddy old pond in a park and I don't know why she keeps going on about it,' said Mandy. 'Come on, Sarah, let's go home. I'll give you one of my Mum's eyeshadows if you like. There's a browny one that would really suit you.'

'You'll give it to me?' said Sarah.

'You're not allowed to wear make up,' said Rebecca.

'I can if it's just for mucking about indoors,' said Sarah. 'Okay then, Mandy. Are you coming too, Becky?'

'We don't want *her*,' said Mandy.

'I don't want to come, don't worry,' said Rebecca. 'Don't go yet, Sarah. It *is* a witch's pond and it *is* deep enough. Look, I'll prove it.' She started taking off her sandals and socks.

'What are you doing?' said Sarah.

'I'm going to go in and see how deep it is for myself.'

'She's mad! It's all muddy and gungy and disgusting,' said Mandy, wrinkling her nose.

'Becky, don't be daft, you *can't*,' said Sarah.

'I can if I want,' said Rebecca and she slid down the bank and stepped right into the pond.

9

She didn't really want to. The water lapped icily over her ankles, leaving circles of scum. Rebecca gritted her teeth and paddled in farther. It was like wading through frozen soup.

'Come *out*,' Sarah cried from the bank.

'She's just being stupid,' said Mandy. 'Take no notice of the silly baby. Come on, Sarah. I've got blusher as well, have you ever tried it?'

'I'm going, Becky,' Sarah called. 'I think you're stupid too. You'll get some awful disease going in that filthy water.'

'I'm just showing you how deep it is,' Rebecca

10

called. The water came up to her knees now and she had to hold her dress up. She was starting to shiver.

'Well, if it's really deep then you'll be in trouble, you idiot. You know you always keep one leg on the bottom when we go swimming,' said Sarah. 'I'm going.'

'I don't! Sarah, wait. Sarah!'

Sarah really was going. She was walking away with Mandy. Rebecca couldn't believe it. She took another step, trod on something slimy, and screamed.

Sarah turned round.

Rebecca screamed some more. The something slimy was only a little piece of waterweed but she decided to make the most of it.

'Sarah! Help, Sarah! There's all this long slippery waving stuff — I'm stuck in it. You know what I think it is? Hair! Hair from one of the drowned witches.'

Rebecca hoped Sarah might scream too and come running to help. But Sarah just shook her head scornfully.

'Who do you think you're kidding, Rebecca Brown? You're a silly baby.'

'Silly baby, silly baby, silly baby,' Mandy chanted.

Then they walked off with their arms round each other.

Rebecca was abandoned.

11

'I'm not a silly baby,' she mumbled, although several babyish tears spurted down her cheeks and rained into the pond. She rubbed her eyes, forgetting about her dress. It trailed into the dirty water. It was her best dress and clean on that day. Dad hadn't wanted her to wear it, he'd wanted her to wear her old shorts and teeshirt. He didn't understand that she'd wanted to look as grown up as Mandy.

She didn't look very grown up now. She was shivering badly too. But now she was in and soaked she might as well strike out for the middle, just to see.

So she took a step forward and then another. It did get deeper. She took one more step and the water was suddenly up round her waist. Her dress was really going to be ruined now. Sarah was right, she really wasn't very good at swimming. She felt very depressed indeed but she didn't want to *drown*.

She tried to take a step backwards, but she got confused and went sideways instead. The water reached her chest.

Rebecca started screaming for help. Nobody seemed to hear her. No one came to her rescue.

'Then I'll have to help myself', said Rebecca.

She tried to work out how to do it. She cautiously waved one leg around in the water, trying to feel where it got deeper. And then something suddenly seized her by the ankle!

12

Two

Rebecca screamed and shook her leg violently. She overbalanced and went right under the water, her fists flailing. She surfaced, choking and coughing, and clawed at her leg. Something was still clinging determinedly, something slimy and scrabbling.

Rebecca waded frantically through the water and made it to the bank. She threw herself on the muddy grass, still waving her leg wildly, but the Thing clung on. It was an enormous black toad, with hideous warty skin and two bulbous glistening eyes.

'Get off! *Get off me!*' Rebecca screamed.

The toad stayed very much on, clinging to her with the strength of superglue.

'Get *off*, I say,' Rebecca sobbed, and she reached down and tried to pull at its webbed feet.

'Desist!'

Rebecca stopped pulling. Her hand hovered above the horny head. She blinked at his huge drooling mouth.

'What?' she whispered.

'Do not look so vacant, child. I asked you to desist. You were hurting me — and that is my poorly limb too. I had an unpleasant encounter with a fish-hook in the nineteen-fifties and I have been sorely afflicted ever since.' He paused, his eyes oozing. '*Why* did you attack me in that violent manner?'

'I wanted you to get off me,' Rebecca sniffled.

'Why? Pray tell me *why*, when I did take the trouble to attach myself so firmly to your person?' He sounded outraged, puffing himself up until his black wrinkles almost ironed out. Rebecca was terrified he might burst all over her.

'Because you're so ugly!' said Rebecca, cowering away from him.

'*Ugly*?' It was a shocked squeak. Then he started deflating with an audible hiss. He shrank until he was a little wizened black ball no bigger than Rebecca's fist. He slowly and deliberately loosened the grip of his sucker pads, took one half-hearted hop, and huddled on the grass beside her.

Rebecca stared at him. His eyes were oozing again. A drop of moisture rolled down his warty cheek. It looked almost as if he were crying.

14

Rebecca cleared her throat. She clenched and unclenched her fists. She nibbled at a loose bit of skin on her lip. Why wasn't she running away? She was free of him now, although her ankle still felt uncomfortably slimy. She could pick herself up and run hard and be out of the park altogether in two minutes.

So what was she doing, sitting here, watching this warty toad, and worrying? Worrying because she'd hurt its feelings. She must be mad. She *was* mad, because she knew perfectly well that toads can't talk.

'Can you really talk?' she whispered.

The toad raised his drooping head a little.

'I have been talking since I was a mere tadpole,' he said huffily. 'I dare say you find my speech offensive too. Pray do not distress yourself. I do not intend to continue our conversation. Permit me a moment to recover and then I will remove my loathly person altogether.'

Rebecca stared at him. He spoke clearly enough, although he did tend to croak every now and then. But he spoke in such an odd old-fashioned way that it was hard for her to understand exactly what he was saying.

But she understood one thing. She really had hurt his feelings.

'I don't think I'm so scared of you now,' she said.

The toad huffed a little but didn't deign to reply.

15

'And I'm sorry if I've upset you,' she went on. 'I didn't mean to.'

'Would you not be outraged if I called you... ugly?' He winced as he whispered the word.

'I've been called far worse than that,' said Rebecca. 'Just now a girl called me Parrot Face. And Stupid and Silly Baby.'

'A parrot has a large hooked bill. Your nose is but a small protuberance. But perhaps I would not care to dispute the other two nicknames,' the toad muttered.

'There's no need to be spiteful,' said Rebecca. 'I was trying to make friends.'

'I was the one who determined to befriend you. I woke from one of my lengthy sleeps to hear you speaking of witches. I was surprised by your knowledge. Moved to tears by bitter memories. And then I heard them calling your name. I could scarce believe it! Rebecca. The very same name as my own dearest long-lost Rebecca. It seemed too great an omen to ignore. I determined to address you. And then you plunged into my watery abode as if actively seeking me out. My broken heart healed! I leaped upwards. With the tenderest affection I attched myelf to your person — only to have you attack and insult me.' He croaked mournfully, his limbs twitching.

'I don't understand,' Rebecca said humbly.

'Neither do I,' he said. 'I am not a vain

amphibian. I have adopted solitary habits during my long, long period of mourning but I have not been able to avoid overhearing the admiring remarks of other lesser toads and inferior frogs. I repeat, I am not vain, but I do have eyes, and whilst circling the pond by moonlight I have observed my own reflection. It is a wonder I am not vain, because I have never seen a Bufo bufo as beautiful.'

'A Bufo bufo?' said Rebecca. 'I thought you were a toad.'

He croaked contemptuously.

'And I thought you were knowledgeable! A Bufo bufo is the correct Latin term for the species common toad. Although badness knows I am not common. I, the Great Glubbslyme, familiar to the wise and wicked witch Rebecca Cockgoldde, the largest, wartiest, moistest, and most magical of toads.'

'You belong to a real witch?' said Rebecca. 'But I didn't think there were any left.'

'Alas! You are correct,' said Glubbslyme, and his hideous head drooped right onto his knobbly knees. There was no mistaking his tears now. His shoulders heaved as he sobbed. 'Oh how I miss my wonderful weird witch, my own Rebecca. But they seized her, in spite of all my most venomous efforts, they tortured and tormented her, and then they threw her down into the depths of this very pond.'

'But she should have floated if she was a real witch.'

'She had a seizure at the shock of the cold water and expired,' Glubbslyme sobbed.

'I knew it was horribly unfair,' said Rebecca. 'But my Dad said it was hundreds of years ago.'

'He is correct,' said Glubbslyme. 'My Rebecca was cast down to the depths in the seventeenth century. I am not certain of the exact date. No matter, all days have been black since dear Rebecca departed this world. I will show you her memorial tablet.'

He puffed up a little and hopped down the bank of the pond. He scrabbled at the overhanging ferns and managed to push them aside. There was a large stone embedded in the earth and when Rebecca hung precariously over the edge she saw that someone had scored the stone with rather shaky lettering. Rebecca Cockgoldde, R.I.P.

'Rebecca Cockgoldde, Rest In Peace,' she read.

'Rebecca Cockgoldde, Rotting In Pond,' Glubbslyme corrected her. He traced the letters lovingly with his little black fingers. 'At first I did cast myself down into the dark depths with my poor mistress and determined to rot there too. I lay motionless for many years, mourning bitterly. But I could not die. Magical toads are notorious for their longevity. And then my mistress slowly sank down into the deep mud and the pond dried out and became unpleasantly overcrowded and I could no longer languish in solitude. Eventually a fool of a female frog festooned me with frog-spawn and no one can mourn immobile whilst tormented by tickling tadpoles. So I swam to the surface and carved the memorial, and whenever I do catch a particularly tempting morsel of dragonfly or whatever, I leave it in front of the tablet as a small token of respect.'

'How nice,' said Rebecca.

'Your vocabulary seems very impoverished,' said Glubbslyme severely. 'Although I am not surprised. I read the potato crisp packets and comic papers carelessly cast into the pond.' He shook his head in disgust. He sounded like a little old man. But then he *was* old — hundreds of years old. Rebecca's Dad told her she should try to be extra polite and patient with elderly people. Glubbslyme was very elderly indeed — and she hadn't treated him with the right sort of respect.

19

'I don't think you're a bit u-g-l-y now,' she said, trying to make amends. 'I think you look very...' She tried hard to think of the right word. 'Very distinguished.'

It was exactly the right word. Glubbslyme puffed and preened, practically doubling his size.

'Quite', he said. 'I do so agree. You will never see a toad even half as distinguished.' He hopped up to her, showing himself off, bouncing about like a ball. He bounced nearer and nearer, bobbing right up in Rebecca's face and back again. She hoped very hard that he wouldn't land on her head. He reached out in mid-air and she flinched, but he was simply deftly extracting something from her hair. A green ribbon of pondweed.

'Oh dear,' said Rebecca. She felt in her hair herself, combing it with her fingers. And then there was her dress.

'My *dress*!' Rebecca cried.

She had been so involved with Glubbslyme that she'd forgotten all about her best dress. She'd been dimly aware that she was shivering but she hadn't quite worked out why. Her dress was soaked. She stood up and it clung to her limply, little trickles of water dribbling down her legs into her socks.

'What am I going to do?' Rebecca said, and she started to cry.

Glubbslyme blinked up at her, stretching his own watertight limbs thoughtfully.

'I have always considered clothing an encumbrance. My own Rebecca cast off her garments on the night of a full moon. Perhaps you might care to do likewise?'

'I can't go home without any clothes!' Rebecca sobbed. Then she looked down at her soaked dress. 'But I can't go home like this either. Oh what am I going to do? I look such a sight and I've ruined my best dress and my Dad's going to be so cross.' Rebecca cried harder.

'Desist!' said Glubbslyme. 'There is no need for all this wailing and gnashing of teeth. I will solve your trivial problem. Kindly remember I am Glubbslyme, ex magical familiar to the great Rebecca Cockgoldde.'

'Can you really do magic?' said Rebecca. 'Can you make my dress as good as new?'

'Of course,' said Glubbslyme. 'If you utter the correct magical command.'

'And what's that?' Rebecca asked eagerly.

'Repeat my illustrious name seven times.'

'Glubbslyme, Glubbslyme, Glubbslyme —' Rebecca began.

'Desist!' said Glubbslyme, sighing irritably. 'It is not quite that simple.'

'I didn't think you could,' said Rebecca.

'You dare to doubt me?' said Glubbslyme.

'Well,' said Rebecca. She took hold of her sodden hem and squeezed. The trickles merged and became a minor waterfall. 'I don't see how anyone could dry my dress just like that.'

'I can. In my own way. Magic is a science as well as an art. One must work it out logically. Now, your strange shift-like garment is soaking wet, agreed? So we have to find a magical means of drying it. Well, that is easy enough. The sun shall come out.'

Rebecca looked up at the grey clouds overhead.

'Have a little faith, please!' said Glubbslyme. 'Utter the magical command.'

Rebecca took a deep breath and then said, 'Glubbslyme, Glubbslyme, Glubbslyme, Glubbslyme, Glubbslyme, Glubbslyme, Glubbslyme,' counting on her fingers to make sure she'd got it right.

Glubbslyme settled himself on the bank, looking up at the sky. His bulbous eyes protruded until they looked as if they might pop out altogether. Then they started revolving. They turned slowly round and round in an anti-clockwise direction, one, two, three, four, five, six, seven times.

And then the sun came out. The clouds parted. There were grey clouds to the left and grey clouds to the right, but there was a brilliant blue patch of sky directly overhead. The sun shone down fiercely.

'You did it, Glubbslyme! You made the sun come out!' Rebecca shrieked.

'Of course I did it. Manipulation of weather. A

mere apprentice task. Now stand still and hold out your garments.'

Rebecca did as she was told. The sun shone down, so hot that Rebecca went red in the face.

'Mmm, I think I might partake of a nap,' said Glubbslyme. 'Do not disturb me until you are dry.'

He stretched out and soaked up the sun, his eyes closed. Rebecca stood still, holding out her frock. It was getting hotter and hotter. Steam rose from her dress. She started to feel very sticky. But she wasn't soaked through any more. She was getting dryer and dryer. And very soon she seemed to be dry all over. She smoothed her dress as best she could. It was badly crumpled and stained a little green in places, but it was completely dry.

'Glubbslyme? Glubbslyme!' She had to shake him before he woke up. His sun-warmed skin didn't feel anywhere near as unpleasant now. 'Glubbslyme, I'm ready. Look at my dress, it's dry. You're *magic*.'

Glubbslyme nodded complacently.

Three

'I think I ought to be going home soon,' said Rebecca.

Glubbslyme blinked, still basking. Then he stretched, snapped up three flies in a row, and smiled at her.

'I always feel uncommon hungry after a slumber,' he said, smacking his lips. 'Right, my child.' He held out his arms expectantly.

Rebecca stared at him. He seemed to set much store by old-fashioned manners so she bent down and shook his right paw vigorously.

'Whatever are you doing?' Glubbslyme enquired.

'I'm shaking your paw.'

'I am aware of that. Cease immediately lest you jar my entire forearm. Did I not tell you about the unpleasant encounter with the fish-hook? Might I enquire the reason *why* you are shaking my person in this uncouth manner?'

'I was only trying to be polite,' said Rebecca, rather hurt. 'Oh well. Goodbye then, Glubbslyme. Thank you again for drying my dress. It's been very nice meeting you.'

'Nice!' Glubbslyme mocked. 'And why do you say goodbye? I am coming with you.'

24

Rebecca stared at him, her mouth open.

'*You* will catch a fly if you do not close that mouth,' said Glubbslyme. 'Pray pick me up at once. And do it with the utmost care, if you please. I require adequate support under the armpits.'

Rebecca still hesitated. Glubbslyme twitched once or twice.

'I see,' he said, his eyes clouding. 'You are still repelled by my person.'

'No I'm not. No, I think you're distinguished, I said. And handsome. And clever. And — and lots of other things,' said Rebecca hurriedly. 'It's just that I don't understand. Why do you want to come home with me?'

'To be your familiar,' said Glubbslyme.

'Oh. I see. Well, thank you very much. It's just . . . my Dad won't let me have any more pets until I'm a bit older.'

Rebecca was speaking the truth. She had once kept a guinea pig and had forgotten to feed it. She still sometimes cried about poor Dandelion in the middle of the night. Her eyes stung a little now as she remembered.

'I am not a *pet*,' said Glubbslyme, obviously insulted. 'Now cease this quibble and take me home.'

Rebecca picked him up gingerly. She supported him under his arms as he'd asked, but he still winced and fussed and said she was squashing him.

'I'm sorry. It's just you're such an awkward shape. Do keep still, Glubbslyme, I'm scared I'll drop you.'

'Pray do not do anything of the sort,' Glubbslyme commanded. 'I have a very delicate constitution. And why do you refer to my shape as "awkward"?'

'You're so fat and so fiddly,' said Rebecca unwisely.

Glubbslyme swelled with indignation and became even harder to hold. It would have been much easier if Rebecca could get a tight grip on him, but he objected fiercely. She wondered about making a little chair for him out of her hands but he wouldn't sit still properly and nearly tipped himself out.

'How did your old witch Rebecca carry you?' Rebecca asked.

'She tucked me within the bodice of her gown. However, I do not think we are sufficiently well acquainted for such an intimate mode of transport.'

Rebecca felt very thankful. They paused to give each other a rest. Two little boys bicycled past and then stopped and stared.

'What's that black thing you've got there?' one asked.

'Mind your own business,' said Rebecca.

'It's a toad, isn't it? Yuck! Isn't it *ugly*.'

'Let's squash it!' said the other boy.

Glubbslyme quivered but he didn't say a word.

26

'Take no notice. They're only pretending,' she whispered.

She *hoped* they were pretending. They were only *little* boys. But there were two of them.

'Hold on tight, I'm going to run,' she gabbled to Glubbslyme, and she charged across the grass towards the park gates.

The boys shouted and the bigger one turned his bike round and started riding after them, but he soon gave up. They had both ridden off in the opposite direction by the time Rebecca and Glubbslyme got to the park gates. Rebecca was holding Glubbslyme so tightly that his eyes popped, but he didn't complain.

'It's all right now. They've gone,' she whispered.

Glubbslyme nodded, still not capable of speech. A woman walking a dog came up to the park gates. The woman didn't notice a thing but the dog started barking hysterically at the sight of Glubbslyme. Rebecca decided she'd better try to carry him down the front of her frock after all. She tried stuffing him down her collar but her dress had always been on the tight side, and it had shrunk in the pond. Even in his diminished state Glubbslyme made a very large lump in her bodice. It looked as if Rebecca had suddenly grown half a bosom. She tried folding her arms across her chest but she still felt conspicuous.

Then she spotted an old Sainsbury's carrier bag tucked in the top of a rubbish bin. She investigated it carefully. It seemed to be clean enough.

27

'You can hide in here, Glubbslyme,' she said, extracting him from her dress with great difficulty.

She put him gently in the bottom of the carrier. He lay limply, gasping.

'I'd better make you some air holes. My Dad says plastic bags are very dangerous,' she said.

'I thank you for the kind thought,' Glubbslyme murmured.

It was much easier carrying him in the bag. Rebecca started to get a spring in her step. She even started swinging the bag but there were immediate protests from within.

She couldn't wait till Dad came home from work. All right, he'd been very cross with her over poor Dandelion, but Glubbslyme was right, he really wasn't a pet. Wait till Dad heard him talk! She wondered about showing Sarah too, but she didn't want that Mandy in on the act. A toad that could talk! She'd heard of budgies and parrots, and she'd once seen a singing dog on television, but never a toad. Perhaps Glubbslyme could appear on television too. He could talk and everyone would clap. And Glubbslyme could do much more than talk — he could do magic. Perhaps he might end up with his own television show. And it was such amazing magic. Imagine being able to make the sun shine whenever he wanted! They could go to Brighton or Bournemouth or Blackpool on a cold rainy day and make a mint of money.

28

Rebecca was so taken up with thoughts of fame and fortune that she started swinging the Sainsbury's carrier again. Glubbslyme clambered up the inside of the bag and stuck his head out, infuriated.

'Will you cease swinging the bag in that nauseating manner? I am in danger of vomiting.' Then he stopped and gasped.

Rebecca looked at him worriedly, scared she really had made him sick.

'Look!' Glubbslyme croaked. '*Look*!'

Rebecca looked all about her wildly.

'What are we looking *at*?' she asked.

'When was this terrifying new town built?'

'This isn't the town,' said Rebecca, puzzled.

'Is this not Kingtown?' said Glubbslyme, his eyes almost crossing in his perplexity.

'Well it is. But it's not the *town* town. Not where the shopping precinct and the leisure centre and the multi-storey car park are. That's the town.'

Glubbslyme muttered 'shopping precinct', 'leisure centre' and 'multi-storey car park' as if they were foreign words.

'Shall I show you?' Rebecca offered.

'I think I would prefer to go straight home,' said Glubbslyme weakly. Then he clasped the top of the carrier bag in terror. 'What is *that*?'

Rebecca looked.

'You don't mean that car, do you?'

'The roaring monster!' said Glubbslyme. 'Make

haste, Rebecca. Run! But hold the bag tightly lest I fall.'

'It's not a monster, Glubbslyme, honestly. It's just a car, a big carriage on wheels with an engine inside.'

The car drove past. Glubbslyme cowered in his carrier, choking on exhaust fumes.

'It roars and reeks like Beelzebub himself,' he murmured.

'Wait till you see your first articulated lorry,' said Rebecca.

They saw several on the main road. And buses and vans and hundreds more cars. Glubbslyme moaned faintly from the depths of the carrier, but he perked up a little when Rebecca crossed the little bridge over Bramble Brook. He sniffed the air excitedly.

'That smell!'

'Yes, it always smells a bit round here in the summer,' Rebecca apologised.

'That beauteous dank aroma is unmistakable!' said Glubbslyme. 'We are by the brook. My dear Rebecca dwelt beside the brook. I will see my own home!'

He hopped up and down inside the carrier in his eagerness. Rebecca was scared he might hop right out, so she pierced his carrier with her hair slide, making him two little peepholes. Glubbslyme peeped and peeped, but to no avail.

'I think it's all changed now,' said Rebecca. 'There aren't really any houses down this road. There's just the shops and the Old Oak, that's the pub on the corner.'

'A fine young oak spread its boughs over our very cottage. My Rebecca used its oak-apples in many a magic potion,' said Glubbslyme, abandoning his peepholes and peering round eagerly out of the top of the carrier bag. 'But where is the oak tree now?'

They walked along to the end of the road. There wasn't so much as an acorn.

'I think they must have chopped it down,' said Rebecca. 'And now they've built the pub in its place.'

'Dastardly rogues!' croaked Glubbslyme. 'Then they have also chopped down the dear old cottage. Oh woe! Oh misery and anguish! I did so desire to visit it once more. I wished to erect another memorial tablet in honour of my dearest Rebecca.'

He glared at the public house, eyes brimming with emotion. And then he blinked. His great gummy mouth smiled. He puffed up with pride, almost filling the carrier bag.

'They have erected their own memorial tablet to the wise and wicked Rebecca Cockgoldde,' he said, and he pointed to the Courage brewery's pub sign. It was a golden cockerel.

31

Four

Rebecca unlocked her front door and carried Glubbslyme over the threshold.

'Well. This is my house,' she said.

She laid the carrier bag gently on the hall carpet. Glubbslyme sat motionless, lurking under the plastic.

'Glubbslyme, are you all right?' said Rebecca anxiously, peering in at him.

'I doubt it,' said Glubbslyme weakly. 'The whole world is swinging backwards and forwards, backwards and forwards.' He hopped unsteadily out of the carrier, reeled down the carpet, and then froze by the stairs.

'Pick me up!' he commanded in a high-pitched croak. 'Pick me up immediately!'

'What's the matter?' said Rebecca, obediently lifting him.

It was strange how quickly she'd got used to handling him. She didn't really mind the feel of him at all. In fact she wouldn't have minded petting him properly, but didn't dare try in case Glubbslyme thought it a liberty.

'You said you were not allowed to keep pet animals,' Glubbslyme hissed from her cupped hands.

32

'I'm not.'

'Is the bear cub prowling on the staircase not an animal — *and* exceeding dangerous?'

Rebecca burst out laughing.

'That's Shabby Bear. My old teddy. He's a toy, Glubbslyme, he's not real. I always used to sit with him on the stairs when I was little, and now I keep him on the stairs most of the time.'

Rebecca felt she was far too old for teddy bears, but when she had to come home to an empty house she liked to have Shabby there, waiting, ready for a cuddle if necessary.

33

Glubbslyme did not seem to understand. Rebecca abandoned her explanation and politely offered to show him round the house. She carried him into the living room. Glubbslyme blinked a lot. She thought he might be impressed by the television so she switched it on. It was 'Blue Peter' but Glubbslyme reacted as if it was 'Driller Killer.' He hopped several feet in the air and landed inelegantly on his bottom, his legs waving.

'What occult trick is this?' he cried.

'It's only television, Glubbslyme. It's not frightening, honestly. Look, I'll swop channels if you like.'

Glubbslyme did not care for any of the channels. He croaked in terror at them all so Rebecca switched the television off. Glubbslyme lay on the furry rug, recovering. Then he sat up and flexed his feet several times.

'Remove me from this dead sheep, if you please.'

Rebecca put him on the best armchair instead but it was Dralon, and it tickled him even more. He scratched. He shuddered. He sighed.

'How about a little paddle to soothe your skin?' Rebecca suggested imaginatively. 'Come with me.'

She took him upstairs. Glubbslyme cowered as they passed silly old Shabby, mumbling about a performing bear that had once broken free from its chain and given his Rebecca a savage bite.

'Well Shabby can't bite you, Glubbslyme, he hasn't got any teeth,' said Rebecca.

34

She took him up to the bathroom. It was a very poky little room and Rebecca and her Dad didn't always remember to clean round the bath or wipe the toothpaste stains off the basin, but Rebecca suspected that it would still seem luxurious by seventeenth century standards.

Glubbslyme wriggled free and scrabbled about the shabby floor tiles, exploring. He discovered an old plastic duck in a corner, left over from when Rebecca was a baby. He hopped around it, obviously puzzled by the shiny yellow plastic. He stuck out a leg and kicked it. The duck rocked crazily and fell on its beak.

'It is dead,' said Glubbslyme. 'You seem inordinately fond of dead animals, Rebecca. Dead sheep, dead bears, dead water fowl.'

Glubbslyme was very much alive. He was

fascinated when Rebecca filled the basin and bath for him. He had a hot soak in the washbasin and then jumped into the cold bath and had an invigorating swim. He floated the flannels as if they were water lilies but spurned the soap after one suspicious sniff.

He could not understand how the clean cold water and the piping hot were conjured at the mere turn of a tap.

'It is sorcery of the highest sophistication,' he said, sounding awed.

'But it doesn't scare you like the television?'

'How could I be scared in my own element?' said Glubbslyme. He jumped up onto the side of the bath and peered round at the lavatory. 'I think I shall try the little pool now,' he said, poised for a jump.

'No! It's not a pool,' said Rebecca, hurriedly putting the lid down. 'You can't go paddling in there, Glubbslyme.'

'Why? What is the purpose of the little pool?'

'Well. It's a loo. You know.'

Glubbslyme obviously didn't so she had to explain, going rather red in the face.

'A privy!' said Glubbslyme. 'A privy inside the house!' He sounded astonished at such an idea.

Rebecca flushed the chain to show him how it worked and talked rather vaguely about cisterns and sewers. Glubbslyme asked intelligent questions that she couldn't always answer.

'I'll get my Dad to tell you,' said Rebecca. 'Oh I can't wait until you meet each other. I can't wait until he hears you talk! I can't *wait*!'

'You will have to wait,' said Glubbslyme. He sidled along the edge of the bath, looking serious. 'I will not be talking to your father.'

'What do you mean? Oh Glubbslyme, he's ever so nice, really he is, you'll really like him.'

'I dare say, but that is not the point,' said Glubbslyme. 'The point is this: I may be a familiar but I am *not* familiar with all and sundry. I am only familiar with one chosen fortunate.'

'But he's my Dad. He's my *family*.'

'I am not even familiar with family.'

'Oh please, Glubbslyme. Just talk to my Dad. Look, he'll be home any minute. Oh dear, I should have started tea, I did promise. Still never mind, when he meets you he'll forget to be cross. Oh Glubbslyme, please, please, *do* talk to my Dad. You needn't say very much if you feel shy.'

'I never feel shy,' said Glubbslyme indignantly. 'And I never talk to strangers.'

'But he's not a stranger, he's my Dad.'

'He is strange to me. You are the only person with whom I am intimate,' Glubbslyme insisted.

Rebecca couldn't help feeling a little warm pride in spite of her disappointment.

'Just one little croaky How do you do?' she suggested, not willing to give up altogether.

37

'I do not think you understand plain English,' said Glubbslyme irritably.

He jumped into the bath, deliberately splashing her. Glubbslyme's English seemed very fancy indeed to Rebecca, but she knew what he meant.

'All right then,' she said, wiping her eye. 'Only it's going to be so difficult getting him to believe you can really talk if you won't do it for him.'

'You will not tell him anything,' said Glubbslyme, jumping out of the water and glaring at her. 'If you talk about my magical powers they will immediately decline.'

'Can't I even tell him you were Rebecca Cockgoldde's familiar back in the seventeenth century?'

'Indeed you cannot.'

'I think that's very mean,' said Rebecca, and she flicked her fingers and thumb in the water and splashed Glubbslyme back. It was only a little flick, a little splash, but Glubbslyme swelled. He leapt in the air and then hurtled down into the full bath, his arms and legs tucked into his body. Rebecca did not get splashed. She got soaked.

'You beast!' she said. She splashed at him wildly but he just bobbed up and down in the water, laughing. Then he jumped right up and splashed her again. She tried to duck but she wasn't quick enough. Her dress was now as wet as it had been when she fell in the pond.

38

'Will you stop it!' she shrieked. 'Look at me! Look at the floor, there's water slopping everywhere. And my dress! How am I going to get it dry before Dad gets home, eh? You can't make the sun shine right through the ceiling.'

'I can do anything,' said Glubbslyme. 'I am the Great Glubbslyme, once the familiar of the wise and wicked witch Rebecca Cockgoldde, now the familiar of the small and very silly Rebecca Brown.'

'I wish you'd stop insulting me. You haven't half got a cheek,' said Rebecca.

She splashed him again and he croaked mockingly. She reached out and seized the bottle of bubble bath. She shook it and then squeezed hard. A stream of bubbles spurted over Glubbslyme. He flailed wildly through the scented froth, spluttering.

'Oh Glubbslyme, you do look *sweet*,' said Rebecca, giggling wildly.

'You wanton little maid!' Glubbslyme croaked, bubbles foaming from his mouth. 'Rinse this foul scented brew from my person immediately!' He tried to turn on the bath taps himself but his little fingers weren't quite strong enough.

'Aha, you need my help now, don't you,' said Rebecca triumphantly. She leant over to help him but as soon as she'd turned the cold tap full on Glubbslyme stuck his fist in the flow so that the water shot right up into Rebecca's face.

'There! That will teach you to play tricks on me,' he said, sluicing the foam off himself.

'You horrid little toad!' Rebecca shouted, reaching for a dry towel. They all seemed to be very wet now. 'And I was trying to help you too!'

'You will soon learn that you will never get the better of the Great Glubbslyme. I can manipulate water in all manner of ways. Cease your silly little tricks lest I evoke all my magical powers.'

'I've got my modern magic too, don't forget,' said Rebecca, giving him a little poke with her toothbrush. 'I could always grab hold of you and throw you down the loo and pull the chain, so there!'

Glubbslyme puffed into a football, his eyes revolving.

'Beware lest I conjure a wart on the end of your nose — or worse!' he threatened.

40

'You wouldn't dare,' said Rebecca foolishly.

Glubbslyme jumped up and rubbed her nose hard with one of his fingers. Rebecca gasped. She could feel something soft and strange on her nose. She could see something large and pink when she crossed her eyes. She gave a little shriek and ran to the bathroom mirror. A wart!

'Oh no!' she wailed. And then the wart fell off into the washbasin. She looked at it properly. It wasn't a wart at all. It was a piece of her own pink soap.

Glubbslyme shrieked with laughter, lying back in the bath water and kicking his heels.

'Fooled!' he chortled joyfully.

'You wicked little tease,' said Rebecca. 'I'm really going to get you now.'

She reached for the bubble bath again. Bubbles blew up all round them. Glubbslyme splashed. Rebecca squirted. They both shrieked.

And then the front door slammed downstairs.

'Rebecca, I'm home.'

'It's Dad!' Rebecca gasped.

Five

Rebecca looked at Glubbslyme. She looked at the brimming bath, the sprayed walls, the sodden carpet, her soaking dress.

'You can't magic everything dry, can you?' she asked urgently.

Glubbslyme blinked at her and did nothing.

'Rebecca?' Dad called. 'Rebecca, where are you?'

'I'm coming, Dad,' Rebecca shouted, swooping round the bathroom with one of the towels.

'Oh Becky, honestly, you haven't even put the oven on,' Dad's voice grumbled from the kitchen. 'Don't you remember I told you to? Here, what's happened up there? There's water dripping through the kitchen ceiling.'

'Oh help!' Rebecca whispered.

Her own eyes popped like Glubbslyme's in her panic. She unplugged the bath water and Glubbslyme started wafting up and down on the waves. She heard Dad's footsteps hurrying up the stairs.

'Oh no! Glubbslyme, *help* me.'

Glubbslyme didn't. Dad banged on the bathroom door.

'Rebecca? What are you doing? Did you leave the tap running?'

42

'Yes, sorry Dad, but it's all right now. I'll be out in a minute. You go away now,' Rebecca gabbled.

Dad didn't go away. He opened the bathroom door and came right in.

'Oh my goodness, what are you up to now?' he said, his hands on his hips. '*Look* at you. What have you been trying to do? Swim fully-clothed in the bath?'

'No Dad,' said Rebecca miserably.

'And look at all these bubbles! You've wasted half the bottle, you naughty girl. Really Rebecca, you're not a baby any more, you're too old for these silly games, and — WHAT ON EARTH IS THAT?'

Dad had suddenly noticed Glubbslyme, who was revolving round and round the bath plug as the water ebbed away.

Rebecca took a deep breath.

'It's my pet toad, Dad.'

'Your *what*?'

'It's my toad, Dad. I found him in the pond in the park. Isn't he lovely? I bet you've never seen such a...such a distinguished toad.'

Glubbslyme stopped whirling. He hopped up on the edge of the bath and bowed his warty head.

'Ugh!' said Dad, taking a step backwards. 'Get it out of here!'

'Okay Dad. He can sleep in my bedroom — and I swear I won't forget to feed him — and I won't make this sort of mess again, I promise, I just wanted to give him a swim and it got sort of wet —'

'Rebecca, I think you've gone completely mad. I want you to take that toad *out* of here. Out of the house. I can't understand why you aren't scared to death of it. You had hysterics over a worm on your wellington boot only the other day.'

'He isn't a worm, Dad, he's a toad.'

'I can see that. And you can't keep him, so stop talking such nonsense. Now go and get a box and we'll try to catch him and then you'd better take him right down to the bottom of the garden and let him go.'

'Dad, I can't. He's *mine*.'

44

'Stop arguing! Come on, do as you're told, get a box. And then you'd better help me clear up this mess. The water will seep right through to the electrics if we're not careful.'

'I'll take him back to the park then,' Rebecca said mournfully.

'Of course you can't take him all the way back to the park at this time.'

'But I *have* to, Dad.'

'Rebecca, the park will be closed. The gates will be locked.'

'I could climb over.'

'Now you're just being silly. I'm trying very hard indeed to keep my temper, Rebecca. Take the toad out into the garden AT ONCE'

Rebecca knew she would never win when Dad used that tone. Tears started trickling down her cheeks. Dad saw them and sighed.

'Come on, there's no need to act as if it's the end of the world. It's the only sensible thing to do, love. No one keeps toads as pets. He wouldn't be happy. He wants to be back outside so he can hop about in the grass and catch a few flies for his supper. Take him right behind the greenhouse, he'll be happy there. Now get a box and we'll trap him in it.'

'I don't need a box,' Rebecca sniffed, and she held out her hands.

Glubbslyme hopped into them. Rebecca cuddled him against her damp chest. Dad looked amazed.

45

'You see how tame he is,' said Rebecca. 'Oh please. If you only knew what sort of a toad he is —'

Glubbslyme stiffened in alarm. Perhaps it was just as well Dad did not want to know.

'Out into the garden. Now.'

So Rebecca carried Glubbslyme out of the bathroom, down the stairs, through the kitchen and out into the garden. She whispered tearful apologies all the way. Glubbslyme didn't reply until they were in the garden.

'Watch that tongue of yours, child. Not a word about my powers, if you please. And pray staunch those tears. They are tickling.'

'I can't help crying, Glubbslyme. I'm so miserable,' said Rebecca.

They had only known each other a few hours and yet she felt Glubbslyme was her greatest friend.

'I'm going to miss you so,' she said, sobbing.

'You are becoming exceeding waterlogged,' said Glubbslyme. 'Mop those eyes. There is no call for grief. I shall bide overnight in the little dwelling yonder. Is it another privy?'

'It's the greenhouse!'

'It is not green. It is I believe a white house, though dingy enough to mistake for grey. But green, grey or white, it will suffice,' said Glubbslyme.

'*Will* it? You'll be all right? You'll stay there all night?'

'I am rather partial to that type of dwelling.

However, this does not excuse the inhospitality of your father. I do not care for him. *My* Rebecca was wise enough not to have family.'

'Dad was only cross because we'd made so much mess,' said Rebecca, trying to be loyal.

Glubbslyme sniffed. He peered about him, looking pleased, although it wasn't a neat and tidy garden at all. Dad didn't often get round to cutting the grass and besides, Rebecca liked to pick the daisies and make herself necklaces. Daisies were often the only flowers growing in the garden, apart from some pretty white blossoms that wound up and down the fence. Rebecca wondered hopefully if they were lilies. She had tried sprinkling a few seed packets into the earth but hadn't had much success. It was irritating because lots of weeds grew without any encouragement whatsoever.

Mr Baker next door found it irritating too. His garden was so neat and tidy it didn't look real. His grass grew like green velvet and his flowers were all so perfect they looked like plastic. But Rebecca knew they weren't plastic. Once or twice her ball had gone flying into Mr Baker's garden by mistake and once or twice a few of the perfect flowers had been flattened. Once or twice Mr Baker had complained to Dad. More than once or twice.

Mr Baker was out in his garden now, snipping the edges of his velvet lawn. He looked up when he heard Rebecca's footsteps and glared over the fence.

'Is that a ball you've got there?' he called, squinting short-sightedly at Glubbslyme.

'No, Mr Baker.'

'I hope not. You be warned, young lady!'

'Yes, Mr Baker.'

'What *is* that you're holding?'

'Nothing, Mr Baker,' said Rebecca, making a dash for her greenhouse.

It was dark and dirty inside. There were a few flowerpots, a battered watering can, several leaking sacks of earth and fertilizer, and a great many spiders. Rebecca had always found this a major disadvantage. She had often thought about turning the greenhouse into an elaborate Wendy House. She had tried tidying it up and furnishing it with an old chair and cushion, and taking some books and sweets and Shabby Bear for company, but she had the spiders for company too, and she couldn't get used to them. Dad told her they couldn't possibly do her any harm. Rebecca knew this and tried to be big and brave but every time she saw something small and scuttling she shrieked.

'It's not very nice in here,' she said worriedly to Glubbslyme.

He did not agree. The greenhouse was just like a sweetshop to Glubbslyme. He hopped out of her hands, jumped nimbly across the floor, flicked out his tongue and munched a hairy spider, swallowed several worms and gulped down a big black slug in

48

the contented casual way Rebecca ate a bag of Licorice Allsorts.

She averted her eyes while he had his little snacks. The tail of the slug hung out of Glubbslyme's mouth in a particularly disgusting fashion.

'Mmm, an exceeding tasty limax cinereus,' said Glubbslyme, sucking in the last shred of tail and smacking his lips.

'A tasty what?' Rebecca asked, shuddering.

Glubbslyme sighed.

'A limax cinereus, child. A naked mollusc. A common small grey slug.'

'It looked very big to me.'

'Do you not care for such morsels? My Rebecca devised a tasty dish of stewed slugs that we shared with great enjoyment.'

'Well don't think I'm ever going to make you a slug stew,' said Rebecca firmly.

'What are your culinary specialities?' Glubbslyme asked.

'My what?'

Glubbslyme sighed again. 'A babe in the cradle could understand more. What dishes can you cook?'

'Well,' said Rebecca. 'I can do toast and tea and coffee and I can make up packets of instant pudding and I can sort of do bacon and eggs and chips and I can heat up meals that come in packets.'

Glubbslyme did not look impressed.

'I will provide my own supper as your parent

49

suggested,' he decided. 'I shall now select my bed.'

He hopped over to the flowerpots.

'I did sleep in a similar earthenware pot with my own Rebecca.' He patted a pot and then recoiled. 'This is not earthenware.'

'No it's plastic. Flowerpots are nowadays.'

'I do not much care for plastic,' said Glubbslyme, jumping into the biggest flowerpot. He shifted about, wriggling uncomfortably.

'I'll go and pick some grass, that'll make it a bit comfier,' said Rebecca.

She ran out into the garden and tore up a clump of grass and then picked a few of the fence lilies. They didn't seem to have any smell but she wanted to make Glubbslyme's bedding as pretty as possible.

'Devil's-guts,' said Glubbslyme appreciatively, as she decorated his flowerpot.

'Sorry?' said Rebecca, wondering if he might be insulting her.

'Devil's-guts. Or convolvulus arvensis if you prefer. An invaluable ingredient in a choking charm,' said Glubbslyme, jumping back into the flowerpot and sitting on top of the little grassy nest. He looked much more comfortable now. He picked out one of the white flowers and wore it on top of his head like a little nightcap.

'Oh Glubbslyme, it does suit you,' said Rebecca.

She heard Dad calling from the house.

'I'll have to go in in a minute. Are you sure

50

you'll be all right?' She squatted down and gave him a special smile. (She didn't feel they were still quite on kissing terms). Glubbslyme smiled back at her.

'You are not wise and you are not wicked but that cannot be helped. You are certain you wish me to be your familiar?'

'Yes please,' said Rebecca politely.

'Then so be it,' said Glubbslyme. He paused, smacking his lips. 'If we conduct our business correctly you should now offer me a place to suck upon your person.'

'What?!' said Rebecca.

'My Rebecca did used to let me suck blood from the upper flesh of her left arm.'

'I don't like that idea *at all*,' said Rebecca.

'How about reserving me several fingers — or perhaps a thumb?'

'I gave up sucking my thumb ages ago so I don't see why you should start,' said Rebecca. She spotted a long forgotten tube of fruit gums in a corner of the greenhouse. There was just one very fluffy raspberry gum left. 'Here, how about a sweet if you fancy something to suck?' Rebecca suggested.

'A sweet?' said Glubbslyme suspiciously, but he opened his mouth and gave it a try. He didn't seem to mind the fluff. 'It's the right colour and it tastes even better,' he declared. 'I deem it an acceptable substitute.'

'Good,' said Rebecca and danced out of the

51

greenhouse, feeling very pleased with herself.

Mr Baker glared at her over the fence.

'What have you been up to?'

'I've just been playing, Mr Baker.'

'Hm. It's all right for some. I saw you playing at weeding just now. It's a pity you don't make a proper job of it. Look at all this!' He wrenched at the white flowers on the fence.

'Oh, don't spoil all my lilies!' Rebecca cried.

'Lilies!' said Mr Baker in disgust. 'They're not lilies, you silly little girl. Don't you have any idea what they are?' He waved a handful at her furiously.

'They are devil's-guts,' said Rebecca. 'Or convolvthingy aranotherthingy.'

'Don't try to be so clever,' Mr Baker shouted. 'It's common bindweed, that's what it is. And it's choking up my garden because you and your father don't have the common decency to get rid of it.'

Mr Baker went red in the face, and started saying some upsetting things about Rebecca and her father and their family circumstances. Rebecca went red in the face too. She ran away from Mr Baker. She ran back into the greenhouse. She had a whispered conversation with Glubbslyme. He suggested. Rebecca nodded. She said 'Glubbslyme, Glubbslyme, Glubbslyme, Glubbslyme, Glubbslyme, Glubbslyme, Glubbslyme,' very quickly and crossly and Glubbslyme's eyes revolved one, two, three, four, five, six, seven times.

Six

Rebecca ran out into the garden to see Glubbslyme the minute Dad had gone to work the next morning. She had woken up several times in the night and listened hard for any croaking. She couldn't wait to hear Glubbslyme's distinctive voice this morning. She wanted to make sure she hadn't somehow imagined his speech. When she was younger she had often made Shabby Bear "talk" until she almost believed he was real.

But when she got into the garden she was so astonished that she forgot all about Glubbslyme for one moment. Mr Baker was staggering around his flower-beds, wincing and groaning. Something very strange was happening to his picture-book petunias and pansies, his roses and delphiniums. Some were drooping raggedly, their petals in tatters. It looked as if someone had been running amok with a magic pair of scissors.

Magic! Rebecca stood still, her heart thumping. It had been *her* magic. When Glubbslyme had suggested blighting Mr Baker's crops with a plague of limax cinereus she'd been a bit doubtful, but when she remembered they were ordinary garden slugs she couldn't help thinking it a good idea. Mr

53

Baker had been so horrid it would serve him right.

But the *idea* of a plague of slugs was very different from the reality. Rebecca hadn't realised the damage they could do. She'd imagined a few black wriggly things, fifty or a hundred at the most, feasting on several plants, maybe one whole flower bed — not the entire garden.

'Oh Mr Baker, I'm sorry,' Rebecca whispered.

He looked up and cast an agonised glance in her direction.

'Your poor flowers,' Rebecca said hoarsely. 'Do — do you know what's happened?'

'Slugs!' said Mr Baker, as if it was the rudest word ever. '*Slugs!*'

'Slugs,' Rebecca repeated wretchedly.

'Look at them,' Mr Baker wailed, lashing out at his poor flowers in a frenzy. 'They're still at it, even in broad daylight!'

Rebecca stood at the fence and looked. She saw the slugs. Hundreds of slugs. Thousands of slugs. Black and bloated, grey and greedy, they wriggled and nibbled unceasingly.

'Ugh!' said Rebecca inadequately.

'Why *my* garden, *my* flowers, *my* prize blooms? There's not a single slug your side of the fence, look! They could have a feast on your bindweed and dandelions but they've not even touched them.'

'I'm so sorry, Mr Baker. I — I'll try really hard to make them go away.'

54

'What can *you* do? Work a magic spell?' said Mr Baker sarcastically.

'I hope so,' Rebecca whispered.

She hurried into the greenhouse and found Glubbslyme lolling in his flowerpot, lazily sucking up several worms as if they were strands of spaghetti.

'Good day, Rebecca,' he said, stretching.

'It's a very very bad day,' Rebecca hissed. 'Oh Glubbslyme, I didn't realise! There are slugs all over his garden.'

'Quite so,' said Glubbslyme. 'I do not magick by half measures.'

'Well, can you magic them all away now — as quickly as possible?'

'Indeed not!'

'Oh please. You've *got* to. I didn't realise what it would be like. And he cares so much about his flowers. *Please* charm them away, Glubbslyme.'

'What is done cannot be undone.'

'Glubbslyme, I command it!'

'You can command until you are blue as a bilberry but it will make no difference.'

'Oh Glubbslyme, please, there must be *some* way of getting rid of them.'

'I cannot understand you, child. You thought it a splendid jape last night.'

'It's not splendid now, it's spiteful and scary and I don't like it.'

'I can see you have far too soft a heart for serious witchcraft,' said Glubbslyme.

'Can't you do good magic instead of bad?'

'One can — but it provides precious little frolic and fun.'

'I don't think this is much fun,' said Rebecca, poking about in the corner of the greenhouse and finding her old seaside bucket.

'What are you doing?' asked Glubbslyme.

'I'm going to help Mr Baker pick up his slugs,' said Rebecca, although she shuddered at the thought. She had never even dared so much as touch a slug before. Her hands shook and sweated now but she knew she had to try.

She left Glubbslyme and squeezed through the gap at the end of the garden fence. Mr Baker was too distracted to notice. He was frantically plucking slugs from petals and throwing them into a bucket. Mrs Baker was on her knees at another flower bed with the washing up bowl. Rebecca squatted where she was, staring at the slugs. It wouldn't be so bad if they kept still but they squirmed disgustingly. Rebecca reached out her hand. It stayed stretched in mid-air for several seconds. Then she took a deep breath and picked up the smallest slug between her finger and thumb. It felt so soft and slimy that she screamed and dropped it at once. Mr Baker looked up and shouted at her to go away.

'I've got to help you,' said Rebecca.

She knew she wasn't being much help. She tried again. It took her minutes before she dared pick up another. It felt worse. Slime seeped out of its back end. Horrible little horns waved at its front. Rebecca retched, certain she was about to be sick, but she managed to hang on this time and dropped the slug into her bucket. One slug in the bucket. Only another 1,000,000 or more to go.

She heard a contemptuous croak. Glubbslyme was squatting beside her. He shook his head at her and then opened his mouth. Seven slugs at one gulp. And then again. And again. Rebecca shuddered but smiled at him gratefully. But even a large toad like Glubbslyme had a strictly limited slug-consumption rate. They needed lots of toads.

'A plague of toads,' Rebecca whispered excitedly. 'Oh Glubbslyme, I've solved the problem.'

Glubbslyme wouldn't speak so close to the Bakers but he didn't look as if he thought much of her idea. Rebecca went over it in her head. The plague of toads would eat the plague of slugs. But then what would happen about the toads? Mr and Mrs Baker would be rid of their slugs and toads didn't really harm a garden, but they wouldn't *look* decorative and a chorus of toad croaks would get on anyone's nerves.

Mr Baker had other ideas.

'The garden centre should be open in ten minutes. We'll have to buy up their entire stock of

slug pellets. Come on,' he said to Mrs Baker. 'And
you, Rebecca Brown, get back to your own garden
and stop playing about with that silly little bucket.
As if that will do any good.'

'He's right,' said Rebecca miserably, when the
Bakers had gone to get the slug pellets. 'I'm really
not being much help.'

There were a mere six slugs in her bucket now
and she wasn't getting any faster.

'That rude oaf does not need pellets to deal with
his plague,' said Glubbslyme. 'He fancies himself a
gardener yet does not know the simple slug remedy!
Fetch me a hogshead of porter, Rebecca.'

'We haven't got any hogs,' said Rebecca.
'There's some pork chops in our fridge, would they
do?'

'*Ale*, child. Beer.'

'Oh. We've got that. Dad's just had a go at
making his own but it's gone wrong.'

The smelly liquid in the special bin in the
cupboard under the stairs had very definitely gone
wrong but Glubbslyme thought it might still do.
He directed Rebecca to fill her pail and Mr Baker's
bucket and Mrs Baker's basin with the brew. As
soon as the slugs smelt it they went wild. They
squirmed and wriggled across the grass and dived
into the foul frothy liquid. They splashed and
spurted and slurped. And then they sank.

'It works!' said Rebecca.

'Of course it works,' said Glubbslyme. 'Let us leave the molluscs at their maudlin ablutions. It is high time we breakfasted. My Rebecca always provided a large bowl of milk pottage. I hope you will do likewise.'

'I've got milk. But what's pottage?'

'Oats, child.'

'Oh them. Well, we've got an old packet of muesli — that's oats. I can make muesli. Come on then.'

They left the bowls and buckets and the blighted Baker garden. Rebecca's tummy tightened as she took a last look at the damaged flowers — but there were still *some* slug-free. She resolved she would be as helpful and polite as possible to both Bakers in future to try to make amends.

'Make haste with breakfast, child,' said Glubbslyme. 'I am famished.'

'After all those slugs?' said Rebecca.

She heated up a pan of milk and poured it over a big bowl of muesli. She stirred it round carefully and spooned a little golden syrup on top to liven it up a bit. Glubbslyme eagerly hopped across the breakfast table. Rebecca expected him to sink his head in the bowl and munch like a dog or a cat, but Glubbslyme picked up a teaspoon and wielded it expertly, not spilling a drop. He edged slowly round the bowl, saving the golden syrup middle until the end. Rebecca and Dad weren't very keen on muesli, deciding it wasn't a patch on cornflakes, but Glubbslyme was obviously eating with great enjoyment. He particularly savoured the golden syrup, smacking his lips and making little mmm sounds of pleasure.

Rebecca idly spooned up a mouthful straight from the syrup tin for herself.

'I don't want to do any more bad magic, Glubbslyme,' she said decidedly.

'As you wish,' said Glubbslyme huffily. 'If you do not require my services pray return me to my pond.'

'Of course I require them,' said Rebecca, quickly giving him another spoonful of syrup to sweeten him up. 'I just want to do some nice harmless magic, that's all. Will you teach me?'

'If I must,' sighed Glubbslyme, licking his sticky lips. 'Well? Which magical art do you wish to master?'

Rebecca wasn't too sure. She didn't have much experience of witchcraft. The only witch she'd ever

60

come across was Samantha in the television programme "Bewitched." She tried to think what
Samantha could do.

'Will you teach me how to wiggle my nose and
disappear?' asked Rebecca.

Glubbslyme stared at her.

'Why do you wish to wiggle your nose and
disappear?' he enquired.

Rebecca thought about it. She couldn't see much
advantage in it, certainly. She decided to try something else. She could get Glubbslyme to teach her
how to make the sun come out — although the sun
was already out and shining strongly of its own
accord, so perhaps that wasn't a very good idea
either. So what else did good — or goodish —
witches do?

'I know!' said Rebecca. 'Teach me how to fly!'

Glubbslyme had forgotten his impeccable
manners. His head was right inside the syrup tin.
He edged it out again with difficulty, flicking out his
long tongue to lick up all the syrup round his ears.

'Glubbslyme!' said Rebecca severely.

He looked a little embarrassed. She had to wet a
J-cloth and give him a good mopping. It was
tempting to play around with the washing up bowl
but Rebecca had only to lift her head to see the stain
on the ceiling from yesterday's bathroom flood. Dad
had stayed very cross for most of the evening.
Rebecca towelled Glubbslyme dry and set him in
the soap rack.

61

'*Will* you teach me how to fly?' she asked again.

Glubbslyme swung his legs and sighed.

'I do not care for flying', he said, 'I suffer from vertigo.'

'What's that?' said Rebecca, wondering if it might be a dread seventeenth century disease.

But it was only dizziness.

'Only!' said Glubbslyme, closing his eyes. 'Once I fell from the broomstick when we did fly to attend a Great Sabbat and I hurtled downwards like a hawk. I was certain I would spatter the ground with my chill blood but my dear Rebecca swooped after me and rescued me just in time.'

'I won't let you fall, Glubbslyme, I promise. Oh please, I'd give anything to be able to fly. Please. *Please*.'

Glubbslyme sighed irritably.

'Very well. One *very* brief flying lesson. First you will need to concoct a flying ointment. My Rebecca used the strongest ointment possible because she ventured far and wide. A weaker lotion will be sufficient for your purposes. Now, as to ingredients. Of course Rebecca varied hers according to her needs. When we did fly over three counties on All Hallow's Eve she did use a goose grease base and added eagle's claw and albatross eye, bat's blood and the gore from a dangling man. I do not suppose there is a gibbet nearby, child?'

'What's a gibbet?'

'It is the post on which malefactors are hung.'

'We don't have them nowadays,' said Rebecca gratefully.

Glubbslyme tutted. 'Well, I daresay we can make do with eagle, albatross and bat.'

'I don't think that's going to be possible either,' said Rebecca. 'I'm sure I couldn't catch an eagle or an albatross and I'm scared of bats.'

'You cannot fly without an aerial ointment,' said Glubbslyme impatiently. He peered out of the kitchen window at the birds on the fence. 'Suppose we keep things simple? Kindly catch six sparrows.'

'I'm not extracting any eyes or beaks or claws,' said Rebecca firmly. 'And besides, I'd get reported to the R.S.P.C.A.'

She made do with two sparrow feathers, a dead bumble bee and the wing of one of Glubbslyme's snack dragonflies. She made a thick white paste with washing powder (because it was called Ariel), chopped the feathers, bee and wing into tiny pieces, and added them to the mixture.

'It looks rather disgusting,' she said. 'It was a very dead bee.'

'Beggars cannot be choosers,' said Glubbslyme. 'Now bring me your broomstick and we will annoint ourselves with your inferior ointment.'

There was a further problem.

'I haven't got a broomstick,' said Rebecca.

'No broomstick,' said Glubbslyme. 'Might I

enquire how you sweep your floors?'

Rebecca went to the cupboard and brought out the vacuum cleaner and the dustpan and brush. Glubbslyme did not understand the vacuum cleaner so she switched it on and showed him. He shrieked and leaped for the safety of the kitchen sink.

'It's all right, Glubbslyme, there's nothing to be frightened of, I promise,' said Rebecca, switching off. 'I used to be scared of the vacuum too — but that was just when I was a little baby.'

'I do not think you were ever little enough to be sucked up into that dreadful nozzle,' said Glubbslyme, shuddering. 'Kindly banish it back into its cupboard. And we will not require the child's broom either. It might prove an adequate steed for such as myself but it will not bear your great weight.'

Rebecca was hurt. She was perhaps a bit plumper than Sarah and skinny old Mandy but she really wasn't *fat*.

'What *can* we use then?' she asked, chucking the vacuum and brush back in the cupboard.

Glubbslyme was peering into its depths.

'What is the long pied stick in the corner?' he asked.

Rebecca realised he meant Dad's red and yellow umbrella.

'It will suffice,' said Glubbslyme. 'Apply the ointment. We are about to learn how to fly.'

64

Seven

Rebecca stuck her fingers into her unpleasant Ariel ointment and smeared a little on her arms and legs. She tried to avoid the little black bits in case they were the bee. The ointment felt uncomfortably itchy. She hoped she wouldn't get a rash, she had very sensitive skin.

'And me,' commanded Glubbslyme.

She smeared the ointment over his odd warty back. Glubbslyme certainly did not appear to have sensitive skin but when she worked round his tummy he grinned foolishly and doubled up.

'Desist!' he gasped. 'I am extremely ticklish.'

Rebecca became very giggly too, in nervous excitement. Glubbslyme told her to mount her steed. Rebecca straddled the umbrella, feeling rather a fool. She remembered long-ago games of hobby-horse, and wondered if she should give the umbrella an encouraging click of the teeth.

'Aren't you getting on too?' she asked Glubbslyme.

'Not unless it is absolutely necessary,' said Glubbslyme. 'Now concentrate, child. *Will* the pied stick up into the ether.'

Rebecca willed as hard as she could, her eyes squeezed shut with effort. Nothing at all happened.

She stayed standing on the unmopped kitchen floor, straddling the umbrella.

'Try harder! Concentrate,' said Glubbslyme.

Rebecca tried. She concentrated until she thought her brain would burst but still nothing happened. Glubbslyme suggested another application of ointment, so she rubbed until her arms and legs were coated in white, and she dabbed more ointment on her face and even up under her teeshirt. She felt horribly stiff and sticky and it made no difference whatsoever.

'You seem to have no rudimentary aptitude whatsoever,' Glubbslyme grumbled. 'I will have to join you after all.'

He hopped up gingerly behind her. The umbrella immediately twitched.

'Oh mercy, my stomach,' Glubbslyme moaned.

'It moved, Glubbslyme! I felt it move,' Rebecca cried excitedly.

'I am in fear that my syrup pottage will move too,' said Glubbslyme. 'Are you certain you wish to fly?'

'Oh I do, I do!'

'So be it,' Glubbslyme sighed. 'Give the magical command.'

Rebecca gabbled seven Glubbslymes while his eyes revolved one, two, three, four, five, six, seven times.

The umbrella twitched again, and then it jerked violently upwards, catching Rebecca off balance so

66

that she shot down the umbrella, severely squashing Glubbslyme. There was one confused shrieking second when they were all actually airborne but then they clattered separately on to the kitchen floor. The umbrella lay quietly where it fell. Glubbslyme did not lie quietly. He hopped up and down, croaking furiously, rubbing his sore arm and bumped head. Rebecca had twisted her ankle and bumped her own head on the edge of the kitchen table but she did not dare complain. She concentrated on soothing Glubbslyme, which wasn't easy.

'You clumsy dim-witted dolt,' he hissed.

'I know, and I'm ever so sorry, Glubbslyme, really I am. I swear I won't squash you next time. It was just it all happened so quickly it took me by surprise. Please let's have another go. You sit in front of me to be on the safe side.'

'There is no safe side where you are concerned,' said Glubbslyme, but he hopped over to the umbrella and settled himself upon it, crouching right up at the handle. Rebecca followed him and sat on the umbrella, clutching it as tightly as she could with her hands, and her knees too for good measure. She chanted seven Glubbslymes. Glubbslyme wearily revolved his eyes one, two, three, four, five, six, seven times and the umbrella quivered into action. It rose in the air — and Rebecca and Glubbslyme rose too. They reached the level of the kitchen table.

'We're doing it, we're doing it!' Rebecca shouted,

67

and she was so excited she lost all her common sense and waved her legs wildly to convince herself she was actually up off the ground. She did not stay up off the ground for very long. Waving her legs made the umbrella tilt sideways. It stabbed at the kitchen shelves, sweeping the biscuit tin onto the floor, and the impact made it twist and whirl. Rebecca and Glubbslyme twisted and whirled too and rapidly returned to the kitchen floor. The umbrella stayed spinning in mid-air for a few seconds as if it hadn't noticed they were missing, but then it tumbled down and landed with a thwack against the door frame, chipping off a large flake of paint.

'Oh help,' said Rebecca wearily.

Glubbslyme said nothing at all for several

68

seconds. He lay flat on his back, twitching.

'Glubbslyme? You are all right, aren't you?' Rebecca enquired anxiously.

'I am exceeding all *wrong*,' said Glubbslyme. He struggled to his feet and brushed biscuit crumbs from his body. He nibbled one absent-mindedly, and then started serious munching. 'We will abandon this flying foolery forthwith. Perhaps you relish the idea of pain and confusion and indignity. I do not.'

'But I can't give up now, not when I'm just getting the hang of it,' said Rebecca.

'You are "getting the hang" of falling, not flying,' said Glubbslyme.

'Can't we have a few more goes, please? I really did do it. I was right up in the air.'

Glubbslyme sighed. Rebecca picked up some bigger bits of biscuit to persuade him. She'd have to sweep the kitchen floor properly and see if there was any way she could stick the piece of paint-flake back on to the door frame but she wasn't going to bother about that now.

There wasn't much point in bothering. On her next flight she knocked the cornflake packet off the shelf too, and the flight after that she managed to fly smack into the wall, and the point of Dad's umbrella chipped a great chunk out of the plaster. That really did alarm her and she tried doing a temporary repair with the last of the Ariel ointment, which proved totally ineffective.

69

'What's Dad going to say?' she whispered — but the feeling of flying had been so wonderful she soon stopped worrying. She decided she simply didn't have room enough in the kitchen, so she persuaded Glubbslyme to perch on the umbrella at the top of the stairs.

It was a sensible idea. Rebecca could kick off and actually aim the umbrella. They flew from the top of the stairs to the bottom, zig-zagging a little and landing in a heap in the hall, but it was proper flight for all that.

'Isn't it fantastic!' said Rebecca, jumping up and down with excitement. 'It's heaps and heaps better than riding a bike or going down a slide.'

'Desist,' Glubbslyme groaned. 'There is no need to bounce like a ball in a cup. I feel giddy enough as it is without your crazy bobbing up and down.'

'Oh Glubbslyme, you can't possibly be feeling giddy when we flew such a little way! Come on, let's do it again. And again and again and again.'

'You do it. Again and again. I will lie here and close my eyes until the world stops spinning,' groaned Glubbslyme.

Rebecca wondered if she really could do it by herself. She did seem to have got the knack now. She decided to give it a try. She wisely did not climb to the top of the stairs. She straddled the umbrella and launched herself into the air three steps from the bottom. It was just as well. She landed very quickly

70

indeed on both knees and her chin. She lay where she was with her bottom sticking up in the air, wondering whether her teeth were still attached. She ran her tongue over them gingerly but they all seemed to be in place. Then she wondered if her jaw had dislocated, but when she sat up she found she could move it easily if painfully.

'Why are you grimacing so terribly?' Glubbslyme enquired. 'Are you having a seizure?'

'No, of course not. I'm sort of putting my face back into place because it got banged a bit. Glubbslyme, I can't fly at all without you.'

'I am aware of that', said Glubbslyme.

'So will you do it with me? Just *once* more?'

Glubbslyme reluctantly complied. They flew from the top of the stairs to the bottom. Apart from one bump on the bannisters it was a perfect flight. Rebecca tried for another once more. And then another. She was starting to be able to steer properly now, and this time she even managed a decorous landing, feet first.

'I can do it, I can do it!' she yelled triumphantly.

'I?' said Glubbslyme.

'We. You. Oh Glubbslyme, no wonder they called you great. You really are. You're the most magical toad ever. I'm so proud and pleased that you're my familiar.'

Glubbslyme puffed up automatically, but his eyes were suspicious.

71

'Why do you burble praise, child?'

'Because I think you're so wonderful. And — '

'And?'

'And I want you to come and fly outside with me.'

'No.'

'Please.'

'*No!*'

'*Please!*'

They discussed it in this rather basic fashion for five minutes. Eventually, when Rebecca had recklessly promised a tin of golden syrup, a bag of assorted biscuits, and anything else in Sainsburys that might prove tempting, Glubbslyme started to waver.

'Perhaps one brief journey across your garden might not be *too* upsetting to my system.'

Rebecca peered out of the kitchen window. Mr Baker was trecking round his garden with yet another bucket full of drunken slugs. It looked as if he was going to be out there a very long time.

'He'll see us if we fly in the garden,' said Rebecca. 'Why don't we go to the park, Glubbslyme? We could find a quiet part away from the gates. And you could have a little paddle in your own pond.'

'I see,' said Glubbslyme. 'And when you tire of flying you will tire of me too and tell me to crawl back under my stone.' He had already started deflating.

'No! No, of *course* not. How could you think such a thing? I couldn't bear to lose you now, Glubbslyme. It's such fun having you with me. I want you to stay with me for ever,' said Rebecca, realising it was true.

'I see,' said Glubbslyme, in a very different tone. 'Let us proceed to the park.'

Rebecca knew he was uncomfortable in the plastic carrier so she found an old canvas shopping bag and slipped her own pillow inside so that Glubbslyme was suitably cushioned. (It was very kind of her because Glubbslyme was still sticky from the syrup and covered in crumbs.) She looked in need of a good wash herself, covered as she was in dried white patches of Ariel ointment, but that couldn't be helped.

She set off for the park, Glubbslyme's shopping bag in one hand, the large umbrella in the other. They were quite heavy and it was a very hot day. Halfway along the road they met Mrs Baker, her shopping basket clinking with big bottles of beer.

'Hello Rebecca' she said, puffing and blowing. 'Was it *you* who poured the beer into our buckets?'

Rebecca nodded.

'I thought it was! You clever girl, it's working wonderfully. I've just been down to the supermarket to buy some more. I felt so silly at the check-out — I do hope the girl didn't think I wanted to *drink* all

73

this beer. It was so kind of you to help us out — especially when my husband was a bit tetchy with you.'

'I just thought it might help,' said Rebecca, going red. She didn't want Mrs Baker to be so grateful, it made her feel worse.

'Are you just off to the shops yourself, dear? You are a good girl. But I don't know why you've got that great big umbrella. The weather forecast said it's going to be hot and sunny all day. It's not going to rain.'

'Well, I thought it looked a bit cloudy,' said Rebecca.

'Nonsense!' said Mrs Baker. 'Here, give me the umbrella and I'll pop it in your porch for you. It's silly to lug it all the way to the shops and back for nothing.'

'I think I'd like to keep it, just to be on the safe side,' said Rebecca.

'Really!' said Mrs Baker, peering up at the bright blue sky. 'There's not a cloud in sight. It couldn't *possibly* rain.'

She set off down the road, shaking her head at Rebecca's stupidity. It was too great a temptation. Rebecca put her head inside the shopping bag and whispered. The blue sky darkened. The sun disappeared. There was a sudden hissing sound. Rain. Drenching torrents. Mrs Baker shrieked and ran for cover.

Eight

It rained and rained. The wind blew hard and the sky was almost black. Rebecca was getting very wet. Her dress was soaking and the Ariel ointment was beginning to bubble.

'I think that's enough rain for now, Glubbslyme,' she whispered into the shoping bag.

Glubbslyme sighed.

'I summon forth a squally tempest but before it has scarce begun you wish it stopped. The Magical Arts are not worked like your newfangled taps, child.'

'But I'm getting soaked,' said Rebecca.

She had often been soaked in the short time she had known Glubbslyme. Perhaps she should prepare herself and dress up in waterproof apron and wellington boots each morning. Then she grinned and grasped the umbrella.

'I am an idiot,' she said, and she opened it up and held it over her head.

Glubbslyme peered out of the shopping bag in alarm.

'It will become aerial. Put it down at once. We cannot fly in a tempest!'

They had no option. Rebecca didn't have a chance to collapse the umbrella. The wind whistled

75

and whirled, and the umbrella bobbed and danced, shook and shivered, and then suddenly shot up into the air. Rebecca shot up with it — and Glubbslyme in the shopping bag. They bounced along about three feet above the pavement, very nearly banged into a lamp-post, and then soared upwards in a gust of wind. A woman looked out of the window of her flat and screamed silently behind the glass when she saw Rebecca shooting past. Rebecca was too shocked to scream herself. It was too wet and windy to draw breath in any case. She concentrated on clinging to the umbrella and the shopping bag, her knuckles whitening. She tried looking down and it was a big mistake. Glubbslyme didn't sound too happy about it either. He had retreated right into the shopping bag and was croaking piteously.

'Magic us down again, Glubbslyme,' Rebecca shouted. She tried to draw enough breath for seven Glubbslymes but it was a wasted effort. Glubbslyme wasn't in a fit condition for magic.

The rain increased until it was a thick grey blur and Rebecca couldn't see a thing. She did scream then, but she hung on valiantly to umbrella and shopping bag until suddenly she was in sunshine. She blinked, bewildered, and then dared peer down again. There was the thick grey blur lapping the soles of her sandals.

'It's a cloud!' she announced, 'Glubbslyme, we're above the clouds now!'

76

Glubbslyme did not reply. Rebecca worried about him. She did her best to peer into the shopping bag whilst the umbrella seemed relatively stable. She couldn't see properly because the inside of the shopping bag was too dark. Perhaps it was just as well. It sounded as if Glubbslyme was being sick.

'You poor thing,' said Rebecca.

Glubbslyme groaned very weakly in agreement.

'You might feel a bit better if you took your head out of the shopping bag,' Rebecca suggested. 'Get a bit of fresh air. It's not raining up here at all, it's lovely and sunny, look.'

Glubbslyme did not seem interested. But Rebecca was beginning to enjoy her flight. Now that the wind had dropped the umbrella didn't jerk about so violently. It had stopped its upward rush and was now slowly drifting sideways. It was much less of a strain hanging onto the handle. Rebecca could relax a little, even try stretching out in mid-air and giving her legs a little kick. The umbrella went gently to the left when she kicked her left foot. She tried with the right. It seemed she had learned the secret of steering. She started to get a little bolder. She hooked the shopping bag as securely as she could to the umbrella handle and then pushed upwards. The umbrella flew up. Rebecca pulled down and the umbrella obediently swooped down until they were nearly in the clouds again. Rebecca pushed and the umbrella flew up and she laughed delightedly.

'I can do it! I can fly! Oh Glubbslyme, I'm flying it! I can make it do exactly what I want.'

'Then make it return to earth immediately,' Glubbslyme whimpered from within the swaying shopping bag.

'But it's so *lovely*,' said Rebecca, swerving elegantly to the left to avoid a startled flock of sparrows. 'Oh goodness, if only I could tell Sarah.'

Sarah had flown in an aeroplane at Easter and had boasted about it for weeks afterwards. But this was a hundred times better than a tourist flight to Benidorm. It was better than looping the loop in Concorde.

Rebecca pointed her toes and smiled idiotically, hoping she looked as decorative as possible. She swooped to the right, she swooped to the left, she swooped right down into the cloud, trailing her legs in the wet mist as if she were going paddling. She swooped up and up and up until her head throbbed and her eyes blurred as she stared at the beauty of the big blue sky.

'I can fly for ever!' she shouted, flying faster and faster and faster.

The wind whipped her hair and watered her eyes. It shook her skirt and stung her bare legs. It seized the shopping bag and swayed it violently backwards and forwards. The handles jerked up and down, up and down — and then suddenly slipped right off the umbrella.

'Glubbslyme!' Rebecca screamed as the shopping bag and its contents went flying down the way.

Rebecca took hold of the umbrella with both hands and aimed for the earth. She shot downwards, frantically searching for the shopping bag. She saw it for an instant, tumbling over and over as it plummeted, and then it disappeared into the cloud. Rebecca steered the umbrella into the cloud too and fought her way through the wet mist. She came out the other side spluttering and shouting for Glubbslyme. She peered desperately downwards. She couldn't see the shopping bag anywhere. She shook the umbrella to make it go faster but it was much harder to control in the wind and rain.

'Glubbslyme, Glubbslyme, where *are* you?' she shouted, but the wind whipped her words away.

She was flying above the main road and she saw the lorries thundering past underneath her. She saw a little dark speck in the road and for one terrible moment she thought it was a black toad and she screamed as a lorry crunched right over it — but when she swooped nearer she saw it was only a flattened beer can.

It frightened her so badly that she lost all control of the umbrella. It wavered wildly in the air, pulling her up and down and once even upside down. Rebecca shut her eyes and stopped caring. And then something punched her so hard in the stomach that her arms jerked up in the air and the umbrella handle slid from her grip. The umbrella escaped, spinning its spokes so wildly its red and yellow stripes blurred into orange. Rebecca blinked, still stunned. She realised she had stopped falling. Then her eyes focussed. She was at the top of a very tall tree, suspended across a branch with her legs still dangling. And there, caught at the very end of the branch, hanging on a twig, was a very familiar shopping bag.

'Glubbslyme!'

'Is that Rebecca?' came a very feeble croak from within the bag.

'Oh Glubbslyme, yes it's me. Don't worry, we're

safe now, the silly old umbrella's flown away,' said Rebecca.

They still weren't exactly safe. They were at the top of a very tall tree. In fact some boys playing football in the rain spotted Rebecca and came running over the muddy grass, their mouths gaping.

'How did you get right up there?' one yelled.

'Oh, it was easy peasy,' said Rebecca, trying to sound nonchalant.

'We never saw you climbing up,' the boy shouted suspiciously.

'You can't see for looking,' said Rebecca.

'Are they boys? Do they have bicycles?' Glubbslyme hissed.

'Don't worry, they'll get fed up in a minute and go away,' Rebecca whispered. 'Then we can climb down.'

She was right and she was wrong. The boys did get fed up and went back to their game of football. But Rebecca found climbing down a tall tree with a shopping bag clutched to her chest a very difficult task indeed. It took her five full minutes to edge along the branch, and another five minutes recovering before she could face the descent. But she bravely did her best, although her progress was further hampered by a bossy woman in a blue kagool who kept calling up at her that she was a silly little fool to climb such a dangerous tree and she must come down at once. Poor Rebecca was doing her very best to come down. She slipped and slithered and fell the last six feet, landing with a hard bump — but she still clung on to the shopping bag, keeping Glubbslyme safe.

The woman scolded her very crossly indeed, although she did pick her up and set her on her feet, and then licked her hankie and mopped up the worst of Rebecca's scratches.

'Don't you ever do anything so silly again,' she said.

'I won't, I promise,' said Rebecca fervently.

She found out the playing field was right the other side of the town. She had no money for the bus so she had to walk all the way home, even though it was miles, she was tired already, and it was still raining.

'Would it work if we wished for some Seven League Boots, Glubbslyme?' she said into the shopping bag.

Glubbslyme wasn't up to answering. When Rebecca at long last got him home she had to give him a thorough bath and hide the ruined shopping bag and her pillow in the cupboard. She had no idea how she was going to explain their disappearance — or that of the umbrella — but she was too worried about Glubbslyme to care.

He groaned feebly, his eyes glazed, his skin dry and burning.

'It's because you were so sick,' said Rebecca

and she tenderly tucked him up in his pot.

He still looked very poorly, opening and closing his dry lips.

'You need a drink, don't you, poor little pet,' said Rebecca.

'If you please,' Glubbslyme whispered. His head rolled and a tear rolled down his cheek. 'Whenever I was tormented with vomitings and pains in the belly my dear Rebecca used to give me camomile juice.'

'I don't think you can get that nowadays,' said Rebecca. 'What's it look like?'

'It's yellow and bubbly and it is very beneficial.'

'Hang on, I know something very similar!' said Rebecca.

She poured him a little beaker of Lucozade, and then another little beaker and another. Glubbslyme drank it much too quickly, the bubbles going right up his nose. He was soon almost his old self, but he hiccupped horribly for hours.

Nine

'Hello Becky.'

'Who's that?' said Rebecca into the telephone receiver.

'It's me, Sarah.'

Rebecca had known straightaway that it was Sarah. She hadn't heard from her since the day Sarah had run off with Mandy while she was floundering in Glubbslyme's pond. Rebecca had been very hurt that Sarah hadn't bothered to get in touch. She had decided that Sarah was no longer her Best Friend. Sarah was now her Number One Worst Enemy. And yet...

'What do you want?' Rebecca asked gruffly.

'I wondered if you wanted to come round and play,' said Sarah.

'When?' said Rebecca, weakening.

'Now,' said Sarah.

'Okay,' said Rebecca.

She badly wanted to ask whether Mandy would be there too, but she couldn't get the words out. So she just said goodbye and hung up. She sat by the telephone a moment, trying to decide whether she was pleased that Sarah wanted to be friends again. She decided she was very pleased indeed.

'I'm going round to play with my best friend,

she said happily to Glubbslyme.

Glubbslyme glared.

'I was under the impression that you were "playing" with me.' he croaked, and he hopped haughtily into a corner.

It was very hard for him to look haughty because Rebecca had dressed him up in the bonnet and frilly frock and bootees belonging to a very elderly baby doll. She had had to beg and plead and proffer many spoonfuls of syrup before he would agree, and he complained bitterly the whole time, so Rebecca didn't see why he was upset now.

'I didn't think you wanted to play. You won't do it properly and go coo-coo and google-google like a real baby,' said Rebecca.

'I am well over three hundred years old so you can hardly expect me to mewl like an infant,' said Glubbslyme, tossing his head and knocking his bonnet askew.

'Quite,' said Rebecca. 'So now I'll go and play with Sarah and you can be left in peace. You can go and have a nice hop in the garden and catch a few slugs.'

'Indeed I am sick of slugs,' said Glubbslyme.

'Well, I don't know. You could have a paddle in the bath — or a private syrup gorge — or how about trying television? You're not frightend of it still, are you? I could see if there's a Nature programme on, you might like that.'

85

'Do not trouble yourself,' said Glubbslyme. The bonnet was now over one eye. He tried to right it but his webbed paws were ineffectual.

'Here, let me,' said Rebecca, but he was in such a huff that he hopped out of the kitchen door into the back garden still dressed like a baby doll.

Rebecca stared after him worriedly, but decided she couldn't let Glubbslyme rule her life.

'Goodbye then. Try to have a nice time. Don't be lonely. I'll be back by lunchtime,' she shouted into the garden.

The little black bundle of baby clothing by the greenhouse did not even acknowledge Rebecca's message.

'All right. Stay sulking. See if I care,' said Rebecca, and she ran off to Sarah's house.

Mandy wasn't there! Sarah's mother had gone out shopping with Sarah's sisters so they had the house to themselves.

'What have you been doing in the holidays then?' Sarah asked.

Rebecca opened her mouth to start telling her — but then she remembered Glubbslyme's warning. She didn't want him to lose his magical powers. She wondered if she could try hinting — talking in a *general* sort of way about flying and slugs and storms — but Sarah had got started on what she'd been doing now.

'And I've got a new Barbie doll, come and see,' she finished.

So they went up to Sarah's bedroom and admired the new Barbie while the old shabby Barbie sulked in a corner. Sarah wanted to dress up the new Barbie and let her take part in a fashion parade. She lent the old Barbie to Rebecca and said she could join in the fashion parade too. Rebecca got bored with the fashion parade (Sarah bagged all the best clothes for the New Barbie) so she stripped Old Barbie naked and made her prance around being a nudist. Then she dressed her up in one of Sarah's fur gloves and said she was a Cave Woman. She gave her a pencil spear and made her have a very exciting fight with a ferocious mammoth (a blue plush elephant) and a sabre-toothed tiger (a toy dog with two toothpicks stuck into his fur).

Sarah decided that New Barbie might like to be a Cave Woman too and dressed her up in the other fur glove. They were trekking through the deep snows of the Ice Age (Rebecca had nipped down to the kitchen and found a bag of flour. She had tipped it out on a newspaper so as not to make a mess of the carpet, but it had spread rather a lot, and Sarah was looking a bit worried) when the doorbell rang.

'Oh help, I hope that's not my Mum,' said Sarah.

But it wasn't Sarah's Mum, it was Mandy.

'Hi!'

'I thought you said you were going into town to get some new shoes,' said Sarah.

'Well, I did. And now I'm back. So we can play after all,' said Mandy.

Rebecca didn't say anything. She clenched her floury fists. So Sarah had only invited her round because Mandy couldn't come.

'What's she doing here?' said Mandy.

'She's come to play,' said Sarah.

'I've got to go now,' said Rebecca.

'Good,' said Mandy. 'What's that white stuff you've got all over you?'

'We were just messing around,' said Sarah quickly. 'Are those your new shoes?'

'Yes, do you like them? Look, they've got real heels, see?'

'Oh you lucky *thing*. I wanted ones like that but

Mum wouldn't let me. Look, Becky, aren't they lovely?'

Rebecca shrugged. They were wonderful grown-up shoes with pointy toes and elegant heels. They were the sort of shoes she longed to wear, but Dad always made her have clumpy old things for school and baby sandals for play. He said that fashionable shoes with real heels were very bad for growing feet.

'My Dad says —' she began, and then wanted to bite her tongue out.

'My Dad says!' Mandy shrieked, and even Sarah burst out laughing.

'What does your Dad say, Parrot Face?' sneered Mandy.

'Never you mind,' Rebecca mumbled. 'I'm going now, Sarah. Bye.'

'Don't go, Becky,' said Sarah. 'We can all three play together.'

'I don't want to,' said Rebecca.

'I don't want to play with Parrot-Face,' said Mandy. 'Here Sarah, try on my shoes?'

Rebecca watched as Sarah undid her old trainers and stepped into the shiny black shoes. They looked a bit odd with her stripy socks but Sarah squealed in delight.

'Aren't they fantastic! Hey, look, I can walk in them — watch me.' She wiggled backwards and forwards, her ankles wobbling.

'Let's have a go,' said Rebecca.

'Okay,' said Sarah, taking off one of the shoes. But Mandy snatched it away.

'*You're* not trying them on, Parrot Face. I don't want them stretched right out of shape.'

'See if I care,' said Rebecca, although it was obvious to everyone that she did. 'I'm going home.'

'You keep saying that, but you don't go,' said Mandy, her hand on one hip.

So Rebecca really had to go. She stamped home in her sandals and went straight up to her room and lay on her bed. She lay for about five minutes but it began to be boring and she was starting to feel hungry, so she decided to go down and make some lunch. She cheered herself up concocting a new kind of savoury Jumbo sandwich (with layers of peanut butter, cheese, and cold baked beans) and then she made a sweet Jumbo sandwich (with layers of demerara sugar, honey, and syrup) and went in search of Glubbslyme.

She spotted him sunbathing in the greenhouse, snapping up flies with a smile on his face, but when she opened the door he immediately huddled into a corner and did his best to look dejected.

'Lunch-time, Glubbslyme,' she said brightly.

'It has been such a long day that I did think it *supper*-time,' said Glubbslyme mournfully. 'I trust you had a delightful meeting with your special friend?'

'You're my special friend, Glubbslyme. Come

90

and see the treat I've made you for lunch. Come on, there's a good boy.'

'I am not a boy, I am an extremely elderly amphibian, and I am not good, I am very bad indeed — or I did *used* to be,' said Glubbslyme. 'How can I practise the Black Arts under your puny protection? I have not caused any disease, death or serious damage since I emerged from the pond. I may as well return to its murky deeps. You do not appreciate me — or my powers. You prefer to play with your little friend. Therefore return me to my pond, if you please — though I will lunch first, before the journey. A *treat* for lunch, you said?'

'Come and see,' said Rebecca.

Glubbslyme wasn't in a mood to enthuse, and he simply sniffed when he saw the sweet Jumbo sandwich carefully cut up into toad-size triangles. But he ate it up eagerly, smacking his lips, and even licked the plate when he thought Rebecca wasn't watching.

'I suppose I'd better take you back to your pond now,' Rebecca teased.

Glubbslyme looked alarmed.

'I ought not embark on a long journey with a full stomach.'

'So when shall I take you?'

'I did not state categorically that I must be returned,' said Glubbslyme. 'I merely stated that my powers are wasted with you. I feel them withering within me. I shall lack the power to put a simple hex on someone soon. Come along, child, have you *no* enemies?'

'I do,' said Rebecca darkly.

'Then let us hex them forthwith,' said Glubbslyme, flexing his four limbs in preparation. 'Name all the persons.'

'There's only one person actually,' said Rebecca. 'Her name's Mandy.'

'Her other names?'

'I don't know.'

Glubbslyme sighed. 'We must endeavour to be specific lest we hex all Mandys within fifty miles. What are this particular Mandy's characteristics?'

'She's pretty and she's very nasty and she's got new black shoes with high heels.'

'That will suffice. Halt, hapless child, so winsome, wicked, and well-shod. We are about to put a hex upon you.'

'Just a little jokey hex, Glubbslyme. Give her the hiccups or a boil on her bottom. Nothing serious,' said Rebecca.

She started the chant of seven Glubbslymes but she felt a bit anxious. Perhaps it wasn't such a good idea after all. That was the trouble. It was a bad idea. Bad magic.

'Stop it, Glubbslyme. Stop your eyes revolving. I've changed my mind!' Rebecca shouted.

But it was too late.

Ten

The slugs were crawling all over Mandy. They wriggled up her arms and down her legs into her new shiny shoes. They spiralled up her neck and glided across her glossy pink lips. Rebecca screamed and tried to pick them off Mandy but she was whirled away by a sudden tempest. She floated helplessly up in the air while she watched poor Mandy writhing down below. She ran to the pond to try to wash the slugs away but someone had tied Mandy's thumbs to the heels of her new shoes. She hurled herself into the pond but she didn't come up.

'Help! *Help*! Mandy's drowning and it's all my fault!' Rebecca screamed.

'Hey, hey! Wake up, poppet, you're having a nasty dream. It's all right, Dad's here.'

Rebecca woke up and found herself sobbing in Dad's arms. He sat on the edge of her bed and rocked her as if she were a baby.

'Oh Dad, what am I going to do? Poor Mandy,' Rebecca sobbed.

'There now. It was just a dream,' said Dad.

'I let him put a hex on her,' Rebecca wailed.

'Come on, pet, you're still half asleep,' said Dad.

'No I'm not. Oh Dad, you don't understand,' said Rebecca in despair.

93

She had tried so hard to get Glubbslyme to remove the hex but he insisted it was impossible.

'What is done cannot be undone,' he had snapped. 'What ails you, child? I thought you detested this girl? Have a little resolution if you please.'

Glubbslyme had retired to the greenhouse, sulking. Rebecca had spent a very miserable afternoon and evening, worrying.

'What's up, pet? Can't you tell me?' Dad said now, tucking her up. 'You've been very quiet and odd today. It's not because I got cross with you about that old shopping bag, is it?'

Rebecca had washed it out as best she could but it was still in a pretty disgusting condition when Dad came across it in the cupboard. (She had had to throw her pillow straight in the dustbin). Dad had got very angry when Rebecca failed to give him an adequate explanation for the state of the shopping bag.

'No Dad,' Rebecca mumbled, hoping he wouldn't notice she no longer had a pillow.

'Then what is it? What was all that about a hex? Have you been making up some imaginary game and it's started to get too real and scary?' said Dad.

'Sort of,' said Rebecca unhappily.

'I suppose it's because you're left on your own such a lot,' said Dad, sighing. 'I don't know what to do about these silly old holidays. I can't get any more time off work. I wonder about advertising for some nice lady to look after you?'

'A babysitter?' said Rebecca indignantly. 'I'm not a baby! I'm all right, Dad. I like being by myself.'

'Why don't you play with Sarah more?'

'She doesn't want to play with me,' Rebecca mumbled.

'Of course she does! You two are best friends, aren't you?'

'She's got another friend now. Mandy,' said Rebecca, and she started crying again.

'Ah!' said Dad, thinking he'd got to the bottom of things at last. 'You were mumbling Mandy when you were still dreaming. I *see*. I don't suppose you hit it off with this Mandy, right?'

Rebecca nodded and cried harder.

'You girls! Why can't you all be friends together? How about inviting Sarah *and* Mandy over to play tomorrow? Do something that's really fun together. Why don't you buy a cake mix and make fairy cakes, you like doing that?'

'Mandy won't want to come, Dad.'

'Of course she will. You try asking her.'

'I'm not sure she'll be *able* to come.'

'Why?'

'Because — because. . . I'm scared she might be ill,' wailed Rebecca. 'She might be covered in warts or worse — and it's all my fault.'

Dad didn't seem to think this likely. He told Rebecca she was still half asleep. He yawned, because he felt half asleep himself, gave her a kiss goodnight and went back to his own bed.

Rebecca was not half asleep. She was wide awake. She lay tossing and turning, unable to rest her head, unable to rest at all. When it started to get light at long last, she thought she heard a croak from the bottom of the garden. Rebecca couldn't wait any longer. She crept downstairs and out into the garden. The dew was so thick she had to paddle through the grass. Her bedroom slippers were never going to be the same again.

She found Glubbslyme just curling up at the bottom of his pot for a dawn snooze, after a night's slug-gorging. (The last of the Baker plague). He was not very pleased to be disturbed.

'I'm sorry, Glubbslyme, but I'm desperate,' said Rebecca, and she started to cry.

'Desperate?' said Glubbslyme drily. 'Is the house aflame? Have cut-throats seized your father? Are soldiers running amok through the streets? If so, I will assist. If not, *de*sist.'

'I can't,' said Rebecca, and she cried harder.

Glubbslyme sighed irritably, but when she went on crying he emerged from his pot.

'Desist,' he said, but much more gently.

'I'm so worried about Mandy,' Rebecca howled. 'I keep having nightmares about her.'

'What is done cannot be undone,' Glubbslyme repeated, but he sounded as if he might be wavering. 'Unless...'

'Unless?' said Rebecca, holding her breath.

'I cannot null my hex but possibly I can try to heal the creature.'

'Oh *please* do! How will you do that?'

'With great toil and endeavour,' said Glubbslyme, and he yawned. 'I will have my nap and attend to the matter after breakfast.'

'Oh Glubbslyme, couldn't you do it now? Please? *Please?*'

'If you absolutely insist,' said Glubbslyme. 'Then I must gather as many herbs of healing as I can. I am sure you are fussing unnecessarily. I expect the child merely has a mild gripe or a pustular boil or two. One cannot make specifications when casting a hex but under your lily-livered jurisdiction my powers are paltry.'

'I do hope so,' said Rebecca.

'I will provide cures for the most obvious diseases and we will hope for the best. Alas, even so it will not be simple. Your garden lacks even the commonest herbs. Your choleric neighbour has scarce better selection, for all he be so proud of his flowers. I can use a red rose to bind and cool, a sprig of lavender for pains in the head, and an ivy leaf to heal green wounds but all those garish newfangled flowers are no use whatever. I needs must hunt

97

further afield.' Glubbslyme sighed again and looked longingly at his pot.

'You are noble, Glubbslyme,' Rebecca said quickly.

'I am indeed,' agreed Glubbslyme. 'You must not be idle whilst I am gathering, child. You must fashion a sweet image of this Mandy girl, thinking sweet thoughts of her all the time.'

'That's going to be very difficult,' said Rebecca.

'I told you there is no fun or frolic to be had from good magic,' said Glubbslyme. 'Well, we must away to our separate tasks.'

Rebecca couldn't get started on her task straight-away because she had to have breakfast with Dad first. Dad was still worried about her nightmare. He chatted to her all through their cornflakes instead of reading his newspaper. He said he might be able to take a few days off work at the end of the month so they could go away for a little holiday together.

'Would you like that, pet?'

Rebecca wondered about Glubbslyme. She could hardly pack him in her suitcase and yet she was sure he'd be terribly offended if she left him behind.

'Mm,' she said. 'Or we could just have a few days out, couldn't we, Dad. You know, we could go to the park and see the witch's pond.'

'Okay,' said Dad.

'I love that witch's pond,' said Rebecca loudly,

just in case Glubbslyme was lurking anywhere near the kitchen window.

She wondered what Dad would say if he knew she'd become a sort of witch. Then he'd really have something to worry about.

'Meanwhile, do ring Sarah. And this Mandy. Ask them round. Look, here's some money so you can buy some bits and pieces from the supermarket. Cake mix. And some chocolates or sweets — whatever you want. Try and leave me with a bit of change though, eh?'

'Mm,' said Rebecca.

When Dad had gone to work she did go down to the shops. She didn't buy cake mix but she did buy a large Yorkie bar, two Cadbury's Flakes, two Milky Ways, two Licorice Chews, one Turkish Delight, a packet of fruit gums and a strip of Wrigley's Spearmint.

Eleven

It took Rebecca a very long time to make the sweet image of Mandy. It wasn't the making of the image that was difficult. That was good fun, although it was terrible playing with all those chocolate bars and sweets and not allowing herself a single nibble. She put all but one of the red fruit gums to one side, but they were for Glubbslyme, to divert him from any future blood sucking desires. She *did* give the chewing gum a lick, but that was just to make it sticky enough to bind all the bits on to the big Yorkie bar body.

She used the two Cadbury's Flakes for arms, and the yellow twist of wrapper at the end made acceptable hands. The Milky Ways were the legs and she cut the Licorice Chews into marvellous miniature high-heeled shoes. It was quite tricky sticking them on to the Milky Way legs because the chewing gum wouldn't always stick but she managed it in the end. She spent ages decorating the Turkish Delight head with yellow and orange fruit gum curls and great gummy green eyes. She used just one red for a mouth, and stuck big black gum buttons all down the Yorkie for extra decoration. It was an excellent sweet image — but the sweet thoughts were a problem.

100

Rebecca badly wanted Mandy to get better but somehow it was still difficult to think sweet things about her. Every time she determinedly summoned up a sweet thought about Mandy she would hear a rude voice shouting 'Parrot-face' and the sweet thought would become very sour indeed. Rebecca couldn't manage very many sweet thoughts at all about the horrid healthy Mandy so she tried imagining her very sad and sick in bed, too pale and poorly to whisper a single 'Parrot-face.' Rebecca pictured herself in a starched nurse's outfit, soothing Mandy's fevered brow, smiling at her oh-so-sweetly. And as she imagined this touching sick-bed scene she stuck all the sweets together and fashioned a true sweet image of Mandy.

It was a very fragile image so she edged it into an old shoe box, and even stuck a few leftover gums on the lid to make it suitably decorative. Then she carried it very carefully down to the greenhouse to wait for Glubbslyme.

It was a long wait. She glanced guiltily out of the

window at Mr Baker's garden. It was completely slug free now but it would be a while before the new perfect plants had grown enough to hide the old nibbled ones. Why hadn't she learnt her lesson over the plague of slugs? How could she have been silly enough to put a hex on Mandy?

She kept taking the lid off the box and peering at the sweet image. The box wasn't such a good idea after all. It had started to remind her of a coffin.

Rebecca was crying when Glubbslyme eventually staggered into the greenhouse, struggling with a great bouquet of greenery twice his own size.

'Are they all herbs, Glubbslyme?' asked Rebecca.

They looked like a lot of very ordinary weeds but Glubbslyme laid them out lovingly, as if they were the rarest of roses.

'I have here All Heal and Balm, Licorice and Lung Wort, Scabious and Scurvy Grass, Thorough Wax and Treacle Mustard,' said Glubbslyme, and as he spoke he stretched each herb into strips, arranging half one way, half the other. 'Flax Weed and Flea Wort, Fennel and Feverfew, Camomile and Chickweed, Pimpernel and Pennyroyal,' he muttered, and he started nimbly weaving them together. Rebecca had once made a very similar little mat out of strips of coloured paper when she was in the first year of the Infants. 'Where is the waxen image?'

'Wax?' said Rebecca.

She showed him her sweet image anxiously.

Glubbslyme seemed surprised. 'My Rebecca did used to make her images out of candle wax.'

'But you said a *sweet* image.'

'An image that is sweet, child. Pleasing to the senses, beautiful to the eye — not luscious to the taste.' He flicked out his tongue and licked appreciatively. 'But I dare say it will suffice.' He licked again.

'Don't muck it up, Glubbslyme, I spent ages getting those fruit gums to stick. Here, I've kept some for you.'

Glubbslyme sucked his favourite blood red raspberry gums while he finished his herb weaving. He muttered a few magical sounding words, dribbling gum juice down his chin, and then carefully wrapped the herbs round the sweet image like a little shawl.

'Attend, ailing Mandy. Thus you are soothed with sweet thoughts, healed with fragrant herbs. There!' he said, swallowing the last gum and giving a great yawn. 'And now I am going to my pot. I do not wish to be disturbed.'

'But is that all that happens? Don't we have to say some more or do some more?' Rebecca asked anxiously.

'I do not know about you, but I feel I have done *more* than is sufficient,' snapped Glubbslyme, hopping into his flower pot.

'But will Mandy be better now? Have we removed the hex?' Rebecca persisted.

'Possibly,' said Glubbslyme.

'Only possibly!'

'*Probably*,' said Glubbslyme, nestling under his grass cuttings and closing his bulbous eyes.

Rebecca crept out of the greenhouse with the cardboard box containing the image. She went into the house and sat looking at it. She didn't feel like watching television or reading a book or playing a game. She couldn't think of anything else but Mandy.

After sitting and staring for the longest ten minutes of her life she got up and walked out of the house, still carrying the box. She walked down the path and along the road, past the shops, over the road at the crossing, down the alleyway and up the lane. It was the way she always went to Sarah's house. Only she wasn't going there to see Sarah this time. She was going to the house next door to see Mandy.

Rebecca stood at Mandy's front door for several seconds, and when she rang the bell her hand was shaking. Mandy's mother came to the door. She wore pinker lipstick than Mandy and even higher heels.

'Yes, dear?' she said, smiling.

Rebecca felt wonderfully relieved. If Mandy had died — or was covered in pustular boils — then surely her mother wouldn't be smiling.

104

'Hello. I — I'm Rebecca. Mandy's friend. Well, sort of friend of *her* friend. I was just wondering. Can Mandy come and play?'

'Well, no dear, I'm afraid she can't. She's in bed.'

Terror seized Rebecca and shook her hard.

'What's the matter with her?'

'Oh, nothing too serious. She tripped over in her new shoes yesterday and took a nasty tumble. She's all right, but she's twisted her ankle and so I thought she ought to stay in bed and rest it for a couple of days.'

'Oh poor Mandy. I'm so sorry,' said Rebecca fervently.

Mandy's mother seemed very touched by such unexpected sympathy for her daughter.

'Don't look so upset, dear, she'll be better soon,' she said. 'Here, come in and say hello to her, I'm sure she'd like to see you. What's your name, pet? You haven't been round to play before, have you?'

'I'm Rebecca,' said Rebecca.

'Here's Rebecca come round to see how you are,' Mandy's mother called as they went up the stairs together.

'*Who*?' Mandy shouted rudely.

She didn't sound as if she was in terrible pain. And she didn't look as if she was either. When Mandy's mother opened her bedroom door they caught Mandy out of bed playing with Her Little

105

Ponies. She was making them gallop across a fence on her fluffy bedroom rug. Mandy was galloping too but as soon as she saw her mother she groaned and started limping dramatically.

'Oh dear, is it playing you up, sweetheart? You really shouldn't be out of bed, you know. Here's Rebecca, pet.'

'What are you doing here, Parrot-Face?' said Mandy.

Rebecca was starting to wonder the same thing. But it was still such a relief to see that Mandy really was all right that she managed a smile.

'I've just come to say hello. Don't worry, I'm not staying.'

'Well, you can if you want,' said Mandy. 'I'm bored stiff stuck here by myself. Where's Sarah? Did she tell you about my bad ankle?'

'Mm,' said Rebecca, deciding it would make matters less complicated.

'Well, what are we going to play then? My Little Pony?'

'Okay. Baggy this one with the pink hair.'

'No, you can't, that's Skyflier and it's my favourite and you call it a mane, silly, not hair.'

'Okay then, I'll have this one.'

'All right. That's Sunbeam.'

'No, I want to call him Pegasus, that's a magic horse with wings. Look, I'll make his wings out of these tissues so he can f-l-y.'

Rebecca flew him through the air but Mandy stopped her.

'No! Horses can't fly, stupid. It's Sunbeam, not Pegathing. Don't you know how to play My Little Pony properly, you nitwit?'

Rebecca thought Mandy was the one who didn't know how to play properly but she decided she had better not argue with an invalid. So she played a very tedious game of jumping over fences and grooming manes, and when Mandy got tired of combing the Little Ponies she combed her own hair and then Rebecca's. She gave her an entirely new and wonderful modern hairstyle that made Rebecca feel she looked really grown-up, thirteen or fourteen at least — but she couldn't keep her head still enough and the new style soon subsided into its old Rebecca mop.

'It's your own fault, you kept fiddling with it,' said Mandy.

'Oh well, never mind. I'd better be going now,' said Rebecca, picking up her box.

'What's that you've got?'

'Oh this.' Rebecca hesitated — and then she handed it over. 'It's for you. A sort of get-well present.'

Mandy opened the lid.

'What is it?' she said.

'It's a sort of doll. Made out of sweets. And she's got a herb blanket.'

'You are *weird*. Whatever gave you that idea?'

'I don't know. It — it seemed like a good idea at the time,' said Rebecca. 'But you can pull her to bits and eat her if you want.'

'Okay. Well, thanks. You can come round and play again if you like. I'll do your hair for you.'

'Bye then.'

'Bye, Becky.'

Rebecca didn't go straight home. She went to see Sarah instead. Sarah was astonished to hear she'd gone calling on Mandy.

'I thought you didn't like her.'

'Well. I don't. Not much, anyway. But I sort of found out she'd hurt herself and I thought I'd see how she was.'

'She just tripped in those silly shoes. And no wonder. My Mum says it's stupid, girls our age wearing heels.'

'I thought you liked Mandy.'

'I've gone off her a bit. She can be ever so nasty at times. I thought she was horrible to you.' Sarah paused. '*I* was a bit horrible actually.'

'Oh well. I can be too. Here Sarah, can you come round to my house to play?'

Sarah brought both her Barbie dolls and they had a marvellous game of mountain explorers up the stairs, with Shabby Bear playing the part of the Abominable Snowman and Rebecca providing real-istic avalanches with rolled up vests and knickers

108

and white socks from the airing cupboard. When the two Barbies had set their climbing boots on the summit of the stairs (Rebecca fashioned the boots out of Dad's brown face flannel. She hoped she'd be able to stitch it back together again) they opened a magnum bottle of champagne (an old vanilla essence bottle left over from a long-ago cake making session) and both Barbies got so drunk they fell all the way down the mountain.

The vanilla essence reminded Rebecca about Dad's idea. She still had a bit of change left — and she poked out all the pennies she could find in her piggy bank. They went down to the shops and Rebecca bought a packet of cake mix — and a tin of golden syrup.

'My Mum won't buy syrup, she says it's bad for my teeth,' said Sarah.

'My Dad doesn't mind. And anyway, it's not for me. It's a present. For a person who hasn't got any teeth at all,' said Rebecca.

They went back home and had a lot of fun with the cake mix. Sarah made very neat fairy cakes with white icing. Rebecca made several fairy cakes too, but then she got bored and made witch cakes instead. She thought they should have black icing so she soaked some licorice in water and used it to colour some icing sugar. It went a very revolting brown instead of black but Rebecca pretended that was the effect she was after. Her witch cakes did not look at all appetising but they tasted fine. She ate quite a lot of her cakes but she managed to save two. One for Dad. And one for Glubbslyme.

When Sarah went home Rebecca went down to the green-house but Glubbslyme was still fast asleep. Rebecca had most of the afternoon to herself. She decided — wisely — to do a bit of clearing up. She sewed up Dad's flannel — not very successfully — and then set about tidying up the avalanche of underwear on the stairs. She scoured the sticky kitchen and she even swept up all the icing sugar footprints. Then she tipped some beans into a saucepan and put the bread ready to toast for tea, with Dad's witch cake on a special plate. Dad was very surprised and very pleased. He looked a little uncertain when he first saw the witch cake but he ate it all up and said it was delicious.

Rebecca was happy they were getting on so well. She risked telling Dad about his patchwork flannel and luckily he thought it funny. She even dared tell him that she'd borrowed his umbrella and it had somehow or other got broken. Dad still didn't get a bit cross, he simply told her not to worry about it.

'I think I've been a bit tough on you recently, old lady,' he said, pulling her on to his lap for a cuddle.

'I think I've maybe been a bit tough on you too,' said Rebecca.

When the cuddle was over she told Dad she was

going into the garden to play for a bit. She took the tin of syrup and the last witch cake and went to look in the greenhouse. Glubbslyme was *still* asleep — but when she whispered his name he opened one eye.

'I've got some presents for you,' said Rebecca quickly and she held out the tin of syrup and the witch cake. 'Oh Glubbslyme, it's all right. Mandy's just twisted her ankle. She's healing nicely and it's all because of your magic.'

'Of course,' said Glubbslyme. 'My stars, child, I am famished. Kindly proffer your titbit.' He opened his mouth and Rebecca popped in the witch cake. He munched appreciatively, stretched, and then hopped out of his pot. He wriggled his neck and flexed his limbs. He had eaten rather a lot since meeting up with Rebecca and the flower pot was a very tight squeeze. He rubbed his huge tummy thoughtfully.

'Should I perhaps curtail my victuals? Would you say I am too stout?'

'I'd say you're a fine figure of a familiar,' said Rebecca.

'I agree,' said Glubbslyme, and he took the lid off his syrup tin and immersed his head. He came up for air several seconds later, glazed and grinning.

'You do look sweet,' said Rebecca. 'Watch out or I'll give you a kiss.'

'Impertinent baggage,' said Glubbslyme, but he did not look offended.

111

'When girls kiss frogs in fairy stories they turn into handsome princes,' said Rebecca, giggling.

'I trust you do not expect me to do likewise,' said Glubbslyme.

'No thanks. I'd much sooner you stayed you, Glubbslyme. Handsome princes are boring.'

'I think you are acquiring a little wisdom at last, my Rebecca,' said Glubbslyme, grinning at her.

Rebecca bent down low, on her hands and knees, and Glubbslyme stretched upwards on his back legs. They exchanged a shy and sticky kiss. And the spell was not broken.